LOVE STORY, TAKE THREE

LOVE STORY, TAKE THREE

Gloria D. Miklowitz

DELACORTE PRESS / NEW YORK

This book is a presentation of Especially for Girls™, Weekly Reader Books. Weekly Reader Books offers book clubs for children from preschool through high school. For further information write to: **Weekly Reader Books,** 4343 Equity Drive, Columbus, Ohio 43228

Especially for Girls™ is a trademark of Weekly Reader Books.

Edited for Weekly Reader Books and published by arrangement with Delacorte Press.

Published by
Delacorte Press
1 Dag Hammarskjold Plaza
New York, N.Y. 10017

Manufactured in the United States of America

Library of Congress Cataloging-in-Publication Data

Miklowitz, Gloria D.
  Love story, take three.

  Summary: Increasingly stifled by her overprotective mother and the demands of her fledgling acting career, sixteen-year-old Valerie comes to realize that she must make her own decisions about the direction of her life.
  [1. Mothers and daughters—Fiction. 2. Actors and actresses—Fiction. 3. Self-assertion—Fiction]
  I. Title.
PZ7.M593Lp 1986   [Fic]
ISBN 0-385-29445-X
Library of Congress Catalog Card Number: 85–16183

For Lisa—my new daughter—with love.

THE IDEA FOR THIS BOOK came to me early one morning as I lay awake thinking about the actress, Michele Greene, who played the part of Andrea in the ABC-TV version of my book *Did You Hear What Happened to Andrea?* How did she become an actress? I wondered. What was her life like? At three o'clock that morning I outlined the story in this book in my head. Soon after, I met with Michele, asking her details of an actress's life. Her generously shared insights and experiences were very helpful in giving my story authenticity.

Chapter 1

I'm a list maker.

I make lists everywhere, before acting class or after; waiting to be auditioned; between takes when I'm working; in the bathroom; in bed before I get up and before going to sleep.

It's not that I don't have a good memory. I do. Usually I can remember lines for a scene with only a single read. But going to school *and* acting, and taking all those classes that will make me a better actress, keeps me really busy. Every minute counts. Which is why I make lists. If I didn't, I might forget something very important, and then what would Mom say? Or Maurie Metzger, my agent?

So there I am in my high school English class pretending to listen, taking down what the teacher wrote on the board, without it sinking in. And writing my list: Maurie, haircut, jazzercise, Mrs. Moffat (my acting coach), library, home . . . when something falls on my desk. Surprised, I look up. Everything seems normal. Heads facing forward. The couple who always cuddle together in English class—holding hands. Only one face turned back. It's this nice-looking guy I've noticed before, and he's grinning at me. I pick up the paper ball that fell on my notebook, and open it. Inside it says, "What are you doing Saturday night?"

Before I can react, the teacher stops his lecture and says, "Mr. Gordon. Unless you have eyes in back of your head, I don't think you can read the blackboard."

Everyone giggles or snickers, and this Gordon guy throws me a dazzling smile before turning back to the teacher. All of a sudden I feel trembly and hot, and for the rest of the period it's hard to keep my mind on the work.

Then, when the bell rings, there he is beside me watching while I'm digging around in my purse for some coins to call Maurie. Maurie expects me to phone three times a day to find out if he has any auditions lined up for after school. But my mind is only half on the call. The other half is on Gordon who, just by his presence, turns my mind to cotton candy. When I look into his eyes, we seem to be connected. I sense all kinds of possibilities.

"I like what you said about Ophelia," he says as my legs finally get the message to move on. "You seemed to get right into her character, right under her skin, as if you really knew what she was feeling and thinking." He smiles. "You an actress—or something?"

"Or something," I say hurriedly as a red warning light goes on in my head. Telling kids at school that I'm an actress usually puts them off. A guy forgets I'm just a

2

girl who acts, and starts wanting to know all kinds of things about famous stars that I usually don't even know. And there's a distance that grows between us. It's as if I'm a freak. So, when I say "Or something" and smile, this Gordon guy thinks, of course I'm not an actress, but how flattered I must be that he thinks so. And because of that he feels comfortable and we talk about Shakespeare and books, and before you know it I've forgotten all about phoning Maurie.

I like Gordon's looks. He's tall and kind of gawky, the kind of guy you might see playing tennis or basketball, and he has a nice face—kind, with a suggestion of humor.

"So, what *about* Saturday night?" he asks as the late bell rings for next period. "We could—"

Before he can say what it is we could do, I blurt out, "Can't! I'm so sorry, but I can't. I really wish I could." And then I blush because it sounds so eager. And why I can't is so typical. Mom's set up this date for me with this older guy; he's twenty-four, I think. My agent's son. And I have to go because it's for my career.

I worry that Gordon might not ask me again, and then get this unexpected fantasy where he's kissing me and I'm kissing back. I am stricken with embarrassment that he might read my mind.

"I don't even know your name," he says. "I'd like to call you."

"Val. Valerie Hall!" I say quickly, though I don't offer my phone number because of Mom.

"I'm Tom. Tom Gordon." He smiles that warm grin that goes straight to my heart, and holds out a hand. "Nice to meet you, Valerie Hall."

And that's how I met Tom Gordon.

Not until after school—after the haircut, the jazzer-cise class, and my lessons with Mrs. Moffat—do I remember I didn't phone Maurie. A sick, scared feeling knobs up in my stomach, and then I reason, *What's the big deal? You called before school, and Norma said there was nothing scheduled. So you didn't call at noon. Big deal. The world isn't going to fall apart because you missed one phone call.* Thinking that makes me feel free somehow. It's good making a decision on my own for a change.

So it's five o'clock and I finally dial the agency. The switchboard operator puts me through to Norma, Maurie's secretary. Right away she lets me know how it is. "Oh, Val! Why didn't you call? He's furious. There's this important audition. Just a sec. I'll put him on."

My heart starts pounding and my palms get wet and my head buzzes. Maurie Metzger is one of the three top actors' agents in Hollywood. My mother has told me at least a hundred times, "You should feel lucky he's willing to represent you. You should be honored! He thinks you've got star quality and he's going to get you some wonderful parts and you're going to be famous and make a lot of money. So don't do *anything* to upset the applecart!"

"Hi, Maurie," I greet him, trying to control the tremble in my voice. "What's up?"

"Where were you, Val? You were supposed to call!" His voice booms over the phone so loud that I hold the receiver a little way from my ear. I can picture him in his office. Walls covered with pictures of famous actors and actresses. One window looking north to the Hollywood Hills. A big modern desk facing the door, crowded with papers and photos of people who'd like to be his clients. Cigarette smoke. And The Man, himself.

My mother says he's good looking. I guess. His eyes are alert and knowing, but he's fiftyish with a slight paunch, and his jowls sag a little. He'll be wearing jeans and a polo shirt and a gold chain around his neck, and he'll be holding a lighted cigarette. He's not supposed to smoke and he doesn't, but he needs the cigarette between his fingers just for comfort, even though it burns down to a stub without a single puff.

"I forgot to call at one like I was supposed to, Maurie. I'm sorry. Got to talking to someone and just plain forgot." *Sue me,* I think angrily. *I have a right to a life of my own.* But my legs are shaking, and the words that come out show nothing of my feelings.

"You want me to represent you, Valerie?"

"Sure," I reply.

"Then don't forget to call *three* times a day. Not once a day, or twice, but three times. Those are the rules. When I took you on, you agreed to them."

"Yes, Maurie." It was true. Auditions can be called at any time, and I'm supposed to keep in touch with the office all the time, because you never know.

"Good." His manner softens. "Now, let's see if it's too late. It's nearly five. Tryouts started at three. Where are you? How long would it take for you to get to CBS?"

Without even listening to my answer, he calls out to Norma. "Get on the phone to Billie at CBS. Find out

5

how long the auditions are likely to go. Find out if they can see Val if she gets there in the next half hour."

Into the phone he says, "This is a role just meant for you. One of the leads in a teen romance series for TV. *Love Story*, it's called. They're casting for the pilot now. You know what that means. If the network picks up on the pilot, they'll tape six, seven episodes, and if the public goes for it, more. It can go for years. That means money. Lots of it."

The adrenaline starts flowing. Tired though I am after a full day at school, an hour doing stretch and dance, an hour with my acting coach . . . and nothing to eat except a piña colada yogurt since noon . . . still, I feel great, like I could run the Boston Marathon.

"I spoke to your mama." Maurie always calls Mom *mama*, even though she's a good fifteen years younger than he is. "She's pulling her hair out that you didn't get in touch. She's down there waiting with a change of clothes for you. Grab a cab and hustle, kid. This is your big chance. I've got a good feeling about this. Norma?"

I can hear Norma's answer from the next room. "They think it'll go to after six. Fifty girls have showed up so far."

Fifty girls! I take a deep breath. Some of them will be new to auditioning and taking the call just for the experience, but a lot of them will be like me, with some good credits. Professionals. Real competition.

"You hear that Val?" Maurie calls into the phone. He repeats what Norma said. "There's time. So get down to CBS and get the part. Your mama's waiting. Do her proud."

I hang up smiling.

Maurie's the best. He's made more stars than any agent in Hollywood. I don't always like that he sees me first as a product, then as a person, but that's okay. He's just out for my best interests. Mom says that, and I believe it.

I once saw the card he keeps on me: "Five four, 110 pounds, small-boned, dark hair, green eyes. Can play female roles from 12 to 18 years." That doesn't stop him from sending me out on calls for blondes who are five ten and thirty years old. I sometimes think he'd have me try out for the part of Godzilla's girlfriend, just for the experience. "Why not?" I can hear him saying. "In this business they change their minds every minute."

So here it is just after five o'clock and I'm hungry and tired and keyed up and hopeful, and I go out on the street to hail a cab.

And while I'm in the cab, on my way to the studio, I'm already thinking ahead. Who will be auditioning? Will Susan be there? We've been friends and competitors since I got into acting, at twelve, and we often try out for the same parts.

Will I be auditioning for the casting director only? Or will everyone be there, the casting director and writers and executive producers? At least if they're all there at the same time, you don't have to try out for each of them and go through all that gut-tearing worry that you won't be called back. But if they're all there at once, everything hangs on that one performance.

And I'm thinking, too, of how *they'll* react. Will they be friendly and put me at ease, or will they act above it all, as they sometimes do, talking around me as if I'm not even there. When they do that, it's a special challenge. I put out twice as much effort to be polite and charming and positive.

My mother's waiting for me at the entrance, a big *I. Magnin* bag over one arm. She's pacing back and forth, scanning the cars, a five-feet-tall, fragile-looking mite whom some people don't like. I once heard a director call her "the stereotypical Hollywood mother—insensitive, aggressive, with a heart of solid rock." Which isn't at all true. For all that she comes across so strong, down deep she's as vulnerable as a child. It hasn't been easy for her—bringing up a kid all alone, holding down a full-time job, and giving all the rest to my career. She's like a gladiator, going into the Hollywood arena against the lions each day. And the only weapon she has is her driving passion to help me.

As soon as I pay the driver and jump out of the cab she's at my side.

"Val!" The frown of anxiety melts into a look of pleasure. "At last. I thought . . . I was afraid . . . maybe an accident . . . maybe . . . but thank goodness." She pauses and really sees me now. "Oh, my! What did they do to your hair? So short! You look so tired. Did you get anything to eat?" She grabs an arm and moves me along. "Never mind. We'll fix the hair. Come on. I brought some granola bars. Let's go." The two of us scurry past the guards to the nearest rest room where I change into the dress and shoes she chose for the audition—an outfit that will make me look "romantic" but innocent and sweet. She fusses with my hair, nervously brushing it this way and that.

"Mom!" I cry in exasperation. "Stop it! My whole life doesn't depend on this audition. I probably won't get

8

the part anyway. Come on. Let's go. I'm late already!"

She trots after me in her three-inch heels, doubling her step because of the narrow skirt. "Now, Val, you stop that negative talk! If you think that way, you'll never get the part," she cries. "You're right for it! Maurie says so! I say so! You're beautiful and bright and sweet—everything they're going to want for the lead!"

"Yeah, Mom. Sure. . . ." I'm trying to psych myself into the kind of person she describes. How should I answer their questions? What body language will reveal the girl they're looking for?

And then, finally, I'm in the waiting room. Mom is outside. She's given me a quick, worried hug and kiss and told me what she's said a thousand times: "Now, just try your best. And remember, no matter what happens, I love you." I'm on my own.

There are eight girls in the room. Some of them are sitting and pretending to read, but their eyes check me over quickly, evaluating how I'm dressed and trying to figure out if their chances are made better or worse by my arrival. Two of the girls know me, and we smile and say "Hi." Several girls sit quietly talking together as I go to the secretary at the desk to give my name. I take a seat just as Susan comes out of the inner room.

Her face is flushed. She's wearing light blue jeans and a blue and white cotton sweater. Tall, blond, and blue-eyed, Suzie looks like the all-American girl. She sits down beside me, and everyone in the room stops what she's doing to listen.

"Over a hundred girls!" she whispers. "Can you imagine? But they're auditioning for lots of parts, so maybe

9

there's a chance. Wouldn't it be great if we could both get parts, like when we did that ABC special last year?"

"What kind of questions are they asking?" one of the girls asks.

"Why should she tell you?" another says. "Then you'll have an advantage she didn't have!"

"Well, tell us at least if we'll only see the casting director, or the whole production gang?"

"Everyone's there," Susan says sweetly. "And they seem friendly . . . at least some of them."

I hear gasps of relief and feel something inside me relax a little. Susan promises to phone later, and we wish each other luck, really meaning it, before she hurries away.

The girls disappear one by one into the inner room and emerge ten or fifteen minutes later. We all look up to find out how they did. Some smile or make faces or show nothing. Their chairs refill with new bodies, and I'm counting. Soon it will be my turn. I try to concentrate on a paperback novel, make mental lists for tomorrow, but fear surges through my arms and legs, through my whole body. What if I bomb? What if, when the moment comes to be bright or charming, I can't think of the right thing to say? I worry about all the usual things: if I'll find the right answers to their questions; if I'll disappoint Mom by not getting the job; what Maurie will say. But the fear is good, too, because it starts the adrenaline flowing, and when that happens, I'm operating with all systems on go.

By the time my name is called I've memorized every picture on the wall, every face in front of me, every girl's outfit, including purse and shoes. I'm on alert.

And finally the eighth girl returns. The secretary looks down at her sheet, crosses off a name, and looks up. "Valerie Hall." I'm on my feet before she gets my last name out. I take a deep breath, inwardly shake out the shivers, and step forward, a warm smile on my face.

"Go right in," she says.

Chapter 2

It's a big office with easy chairs and sofas around the sides and a desk at one end. "Hi," I say shyly, uncertain where to go.

A woman comes forward. She's in her forties and has straight gray hair that hangs to her shoulders, and bangs. "I'm Claire Berger, the casting director," she says in a pleasant way, and then introduces the others before showing me to a chair. I sit down and fold my hands in my lap, but the air-conditioning is on too high and it's hard not to shiver.

Most of the people appear friendly, but two immediately strike me as hostile. The first is a woman who studies me with the interest she might give a rack of used clothes. The second is the producer who sits behind the desk, with arms crossed over his chest, staring into space. I wonder if he's just bored or if he's already made up his mind about who he wants, and is enduring the remaining auditions out of duty.

"All right, dear, let's begin," Ms. Berger says. "Will you give us your name, tell us who is your agent, and then say something about yourself and your experience."

They are trying to put me at ease. That's good. It gives them a chance to see me as a person, not just the girl in the part they want to fill. I've been through this lots of times, so it's not threatening. But this time I want to say something new . . . something that will jar the producer into really seeing me.

"My name is Valerie Hall, Val for short, and my agent is Maurie Metzger." I make eye contact with each of them. "I guess you could call me the typical Hollywood brat . . . born and bred here, trained since I could walk in anything that might help get me a part—you know, ballet, gymnastics, horseback riding. Even . . . playing the violin." I pause, then add, "In case I get the chance to play Tevye, in *Fiddler on the Roof*." The idea is so outrageous that even I giggle while the others smile or laugh outright. The producer is watching me now.

"Are you from an acting family, Valerie?" the casting director asks next.

I hesitate. It's a question I've been asked before and always answer with a no. Mom says there's no reason to tell about my father who walked out on us when I was two.

"My father is an actor," I say, surprising myself. "Ronald Hall. Played in some of the sixties rock 'n' roll films." The loose, extemporaneous ease of a moment ago is gone.

No one seems to recognize the name.

"He lives back east. Plays summer stock and little

theater. Not very successful." The scrapbook I keep with clippings about Dad flashes across the screen of my mind. "You couldn't say his acting had any influence on me."

"I see," Ms. Berger says. She smiles encouragingly. "Can you tell me why you want to be an actress?"

Again I feel off balance. Again it's a question I've answered before but always with the words Mom and my acting coach have worked out for me. "You certainly don't tell them that it's for the fame or the money," they warn. "You tell them what they want to hear— that you act because it's the only thing you ever wanted to do, because it's as necessary to you as fresh air or sunshine."

But is that true? I never stop to think. Now I find myself wondering how I really feel, if I really like what I do. Yes, it's flattering when people sometimes recognize me and want my autograph. Yes, it's nice to make my own money, even though most of it goes into a special fund for when I'm twenty-one. But . . .

"Valerie?"

"I'm thinking." I smile and clasp my hands between my knees, leaning forward. "I do like acting. It's terribly hard, but it's fun too. Though sometimes I feel as if my life is too programmed. I wish I had more time to myself, there are so many other things I haven't tried. . . . Then, there are times like when I suddenly understand a character I'm playing and *become* her and something magic happens. Then I wouldn't want to be doing anything else. Could there be anything better than the chance to live not one life but hundreds?"

I bite my lip, certain I've blown it. Everyone is watching me, attentive but silent, even the lady who seemed so bored, even the producer. I glance down at my hands.

"Thank you, dear. Now, I wonder if you'll read these lines with me." Ms. Berger picks up a script folded to a particular page. "You can get up and walk around if you like. You'll read Andrea's part and I'll feed you the other lines." She holds the script out to me. "Would you like to glance over the scene for a moment?"

When I first started auditioning, I would freeze if I had to read a script cold. But not anymore. Years of work with Moffat cured me, and I can read a new part almost as well as if I had studied it for an hour. Producers like actors who can do that.

I take the script. "I'll read cold."

"Good."

She explains, first, what the series is to be about, and the kind of girl Andrea is. Each weekly episode will be a whole story, with continuing characters. Generally it will be kind of like *Dynasty* or *Dallas* except that the characters will be teens, and the conflicts will take place in a high school setting. Andrea is a "nice" girl, like Crystal in *Dynasty*. The viewers will root for her getting the boy she really loves, but there will always be girls or situations that will oppose what she wants.

"Now," Ms. Berger says, "in this particular scene she meets Brian for the first time. Everything she's heard about him makes her distrust him—that all the girls find him attractive, that he's always played the field— but she's attracted to him against her will." She pauses. "Do you get the picture?"

I nod.

"All right. Let's give it a try. Now, in this scene Andrea comes into the auditorium and is waved to an empty seat alongside her best friend, Marissa. The seat is also right next to Brian. She smiles politely at him, sits down, but then he says . . ."

For the next five minutes we play the scene together. Berger feeds me Marissa's lines and I respond, then Brian's. It takes quick emotional switching. Answering Marissa is easy. She's a best friend. My tone is happy, warm, relaxed. But reacting to Brian is another thing. That's more complicated. I try to show a combination of attraction, politeness, irritation at his teasing and baiting, a sense of being out of my depth. As he flusters me further, it's natural for me to answer Marissa differently too.

I really get into the part, changing the way I sit, even the tension in my neck and shoulders as I turn in Brian's direction. I allow my feelings to show in my eyes and lips as well as in how I speak my lines.

Ms. Berger laughs when it's over. "You're very convincing. You must have met that kind of young man before, Valerie."

I smile noncommittally. What I know about men would bore a fifth-grader. What little I know comes entirely from reading books, seeing movies, listening to my mother on the subject—and from probably distorted fantasies of my own. In short, my imaginary ideal love would be someone who has the intelligence of Dustin Hoffman, the animal appeal of Burt Reynolds, the romantic tenderness of Robert Redford, and the looks of—my father.

"Thank you, Valerie," Ms. Berger says, and the others

nod dismissal and bend their heads to make notes. "We'll let you know."

I feel a little vulnerable now, still in Andrea's mode, not completely back to the real me, and mumble my thanks. Leaving, I try to read the various faces—my mother I know will ask about that—but it's futile. The warmest smiles mean nothing. Even Maurie says so. "They take you to lunch and put an arm around your shoulders and with the greatest sincerity promise that you've got the part. And that's the last you ever hear from them . . ."

So be it. I tried.

Suddenly I'm tired and cold. I make my way through the waiting room, conscious that anxious eyes are trying to read how I did, but too self-absorbed to care. Mom is waiting outside, eyes on the door. She leaps immediately to her feet and throws a sweater around my shoulders.

"For heaven's sake! What are they trying to do? Give you pneumonia? I should have brought you something with sleeves! How did it go? What did they say? Did you know anyone? Did they seem interested? Tell me everything."

She takes me by the elbow and shepherds me to the parking lot and our five-year-old Toyota. She opens the car doors while I stand, still dazed, like a puppet waiting to be given life. She chatters on compulsively— comments on the other girls who tried out for parts before me, asks the same questions but does not expect answers. I sink down into the vinyl bucket seat, close my eyes, and let her words wash over me.

It isn't until we're home and I've devoured a big salad

and am almost through eating chicken tarragon and vegetables that I begin to feel myself again. Now I can tell her all the details of the audition, even what I said about my father.

"You told them about Ronnie?" Her lips are tight, her eyes hurt.

"Yes." I sip a glass of sweet, cold buttermilk and look away.

"*Why?*"

I shrug.

"Did he have anything to do with your life? Did he send money all these years? Was he here when you got sick? He had no influence on your life whatever!"

"I know. That's what I told them."

"Then *why?* Why even mention him?"

I open my mouth and close it. Mom doesn't know how often I think of Dad, wonder about him. I don't want to hurt her.

"That *man!* He can still get to me! I wish I'd never met him, never married him! But I was so impressionable. No older than you, really, and he seemed so suave, so worldly. And an *actor!*"

I have heard these words before, many times, and they hardly touch me anymore, but for Mother it's as if she's telling it for the first time. Her hands are clenched. A tear slides down her cheek. I get up to stand behind her chair and wrap my arms around her. After a while she turns back and smiles up at me, touching my face. "Never mind. At least something good came of it. At least I have *you!* Now sit down and let me tell you what Maurie said about the series."

I pick up an orange, toss it in the air a couple of times,

then sit down again. I bite into the skin to make an opening, and start pulling at the peel.

"You'll ruin your nails," Mom says, handing me a knife. "There's a big market now for teenage soap operas in *prime time*, Maurie says. He's seen the script and thinks it's a winner. Do you realize you can collect residuals for years, even after the series ends? You get the part and we're on easy street. No more uncertainty. No more having to rush around to tryouts every other day. We'll have it made."

I pull out the tiny folded center of the navel orange, examine its perfection, and pop it into my mouth. Mouth full, I say, "*If* I get the part. *If* the pilot is bought by the network. *If* the network wants me to stay on to do the series. *If* the series takes off. Lots of *ifs*, Mom."

"Don't talk with your mouth full." My words seem to bypass her ears because she says, "Of course, it will be easier when you graduate in a few months. Then you won't have those hours of school each day too. You wait and see, Val. It will be wonderful! If you get the role, maybe we'll go off to Europe for a few weeks. Then, in September, you'll be refreshed and all ready to give it your best."

"What about college?" Last fall I applied to three schools, two on the West Coast and one on the East, though Mom doesn't know about the third. At the time not much was happening in my career. Mom had said, "Oh, go ahead. Apply. Why not."

"Valerie, honey," Mom says now. "It's not even a question. You get into a long-running series, you don't turn it down. Not for anything."

I put down the orange; it doesn't interest me anymore. I'm not even that sure I want college, but these last months the idea of it has somehow taken root. I imagine enrolling in philosophy or anthropology classes, not just in courses that will help make me a better actress. I picture meeting all kinds of different people, not just kids who want to be in theater. I find the idea of being on my own, away from Mom, terribly exciting. I could make my own decisions, even my own mistakes. And I picture maybe seeing Dad sometimes. Especially if I go east to school.

Mom must read the way I'm feeling, because she gives me an especially warm hug. "Don't start brooding, hon. Nothing's settled. Nothing's sure. We'll decide what's best when the time comes."

For some reason I don't quite understand I want to cry.

Chapter 3

I've almost forgotten about the audition yesterday. I've tried out for so many parts, most of which I didn't get, that it's a waste of time to worry and hope about what probably won't happen.

What I'm thinking about instead is Tom Gordon. As I walk along the halls between classes, every tall male with reddish-brown hair makes my heart jump, and I find myself counting the minutes to English class. When I get there, I do what I've never done before—linger outside, pretending to be killing time, but eyeing everyone walking by.

I see him coming down the hall before he sees me, and my face gets hot. Then, angry with myself for behaving like an idiot, I gather up my books and start into the room. Only, he's seen me, and in a moment he's right beside me.

"Hi . . ." He puts one hand on the wall behind my head in a way that is both intimate and protective.

It's so stupid. I've played romantic roles dozens of times and never felt like this before—all warm inside and fuzzy-headed and happy and scared at the same time.

"Hi . . ." I manage to say. A brilliant answer.

"Were you waiting for me?"

I laugh, confused. He's teasing me and I can't think of a clever answer. "Actually," I say a beat late, "I'm waiting for an incoming flight from Tokyo."

"Ah-*ha*."

We smile at each other, and I like his eyes—brown with golden flecks and a lot of submerged laughter.

"Did anyone ever tell you you have very pretty green eyes?" he asks softly.

My legs weaken. "Did anyone ever tell you you're full of blarney?"

He chuckles. "Why aren't you free Saturday night? Can't you get out of whatever it is?"

"I really can't," I say with regret. Maurie's son Josh is probably no happier about taking me out than I am about going with him. But Maurie and my mother cooked up the arrangement that he's to escort me to a premiere. I need to be seen at these things, they say. You get known that way. The cameras pick up everyone coming into the theater.

"Ah . . ." Tom says sadly. "Here I am trying to impress you with my intellectual depth by reserving tickets for *Hamlet* . . ."

"*Hamlet*? Where?" I love Shakespeare's plays and keep pretty much in touch with what's playing in L.A.

22

theaters. As far as I can recall, no one's doing *Hamlet*.

"You do attend high school here?"

A caution light goes on in my head. "Why?"

"I didn't think anyone could have missed the posters or the constant announcements. They're doing *Hamlet* Friday and Saturday nights. In fact, I was thinking just yesterday that you should have tried out. You would have been great as Ophelia."

"You flatter me, sir." I curtsy prettily and think how very little of me is part of the school. I go to classes and tune out everything else. And when I'm in a production, I don't even go to classes—at least not here. I'm tutored on the set for three hours a day, like the rest of the "child" actors.

"If you can't make it Saturday . . . and at the risk of coming on too strong too fast . . . would you like to come to the basketball game Friday and see me play? I promise to score ten points, just for you."

This is wonderful. I can't believe how great it feels. Sure, I've dated before, but no one ever spoke to me like that—except boys playing romantic parts opposite me, and that was acting. I gaze up at Tom hardly able to hide my delight.

"Friday . . . Friday . . ." I search my mental lists for what's on Friday. "What time?"

"Three to five." He seems puzzled that I don't know when after-school sports events go on. "Then afterward I thought we could go out for a 'burger or pizza or something."

Three to five. That's when I'm in jazzercise and with Moffat, my acting coach. Could I possibly skip this once? Maybe the jazzercise, but not the Moffat. Mom would find out. My ironclad schedule traps me. Disappointment must show on my face because Tom says, "You can't come."

"No." I hesitate. "I have to . . . work."

"Oh!" His eyes brighten. "Let me guess. You're a model. An actress. No? A dog walker."

I laugh uneasily. "I really do wish, but—tell you what. I'll come for the first hour."

"I won't even be able to break away to say hi . . ."

The bell rings and we both look up. He shrugs. "Oh, well, it's a start. I guess I'll just have to make those ten points in the first half."

When I ask Mom about skipping Moffat's class Friday so I can go out with Tom afterward, she says, "Absolutely not. Her time is money, Val! What's she supposed to do, lose the income from your lesson just so you can go to a game that won't mean a thing to you next week? For heaven's sake! Where are your priorities? He's a kid . . . this Gordon boy—probably no older than you are. You've got bigger things to look ahead to in your life than a teenage basketball player!"

"We could *pay* Moffat for the hour, Mom. Just this once. Please!"

For a moment I think Mom understands, because her eyes soften and she takes my hand. "I know how you feel, honey. I was sixteen once, too, remember? It is hard. You have so little time to live the way other girls your age do. But you're not the average girl. You're special. You're talented and ambitious, and you have an incredible career ahead if you work hard and listen to Maurie. Believe me. You'll have all the time in the world to fall in love. You're *only* sixteen."

24

Sixteen is when Mom fell in love. She married at seventeen and had me less than a year later. Why doesn't *she* understand? My throat knobs up and I don't answer. She's always right; she always gets her way. *But not this time*, I want to cry. With or without her permission, I'm going to that game. I'm going to see what it's like to be normal for a change, to have a real boyfriend.

It's just amazing how many things I'm ignorant of because my life has been so narrow. While other girls have been following football and soccer and other sports, I've been busy learning how to apply makeup better and how to walk like a preteen, a teen, a middle-aged woman, and an old lady. I have only the vaguest idea of how basketball is played. I've never even sat through a game, not even on TV. What fun it's going to be "going" with someone. Think of all the firsts: walking hand in hand, talking on the phone, going places together, sharing friends, learning about sports—kissing!

The night before, I'm so excited, I can hardly sleep. Mostly I'm afraid to even look at Mom. She knows me so well, she can read my mind even before a thought takes shape.

Right after English on Friday I run off to a phone booth to make the usual call to the agency. Tom thinks I'm just checking in to find out when I'm needed at my job. I've told him I take phone calls at a nurse's registry. Two lies in one day. I don't like it at all.

"Which agency?" he asked. "My mom's a nurse."

Without thinking, I said, "The Metzger Agency," and glanced away. He nodded as if he knew of it.

"Hi, Norma," I say when I reach the office. "Anything doing?" Tom is standing nearby, and there's a lot of noise in the hall.

"Not a thing. It's real quiet."

"Nothing yet on the *Love Story* tryout?" I lower my voice so Tom won't hear.

"Nope, but we should hear soon. Maurie's doing lunch, but he said to tell you to keep in touch. There might be word later."

Doing lunch. After all these years it still strikes me as false. Nobody in Hollywood ever *eats* lunch or is *out to* lunch. They *do* lunch. They never *go* to a meeting or *have* a meeting. They "take" a meeting. "Okay," I say, smiling at Tom. "I'll check again when I get home."

When I hang up, I feel like dancing. I'm free until six-thirty, when Mom expects me. I'm free to go to the basketball game and sit with other kids I see all the time and hardly ever get a chance to talk with. I'm free to go off for an hour after the game with a boy I really like and who I think likes me. The only problem is, I'm doing it without telling Mom. But I push the unfamiliar feeling of guilt away and tell Tom that I'm staying to see the whole game. His eyes light up, and he lets out a wild yelp of joy.

The gym is filling up when I get there. I climb over dozens of feet to the place Tom said to sit, and feel excited and self-conscious. I transferred to the school two years ago and haven't really made friends. Who has time? Oh, I know people by sight or name and even to talk to, but usually I'm rushing off to special classes after school, or I'm gone for a couple of days here and there, which doesn't exactly make it easy to hold friends. Besides, when kids find out that I'm an actress, they get all curious and awkward and treat me like a museum piece.

I sit down next to a girl in my French class who's talking to another girl beside her. The room is very noisy; it's a hollow kind of noise because the gym is so large. A couple of boys are running over the court, then stopping suddenly so their sneakers screech on the polished wood. A teacher stops them.

The girl beside me turns around. "Hi! You're Valerie, aren't you? I'm Betsy. We're in French together."

"Hi!" I give her a big smile, so glad to have someone talk to me.

"You're absent a lot," she announces. "Do you have to go visit your father or something? Some of my friends have to live in two different places because of their parents' divorce."

"Not exactly."

The girl beside her leans forward so she can be included in our conversation. "You're an actress, aren't you? Didn't you play in some after-school special?"

I go wary and nod.

"Is that why you're not in school regularly? You have to work?"

"Yes, sometimes."

"Well, gee . . . it must be such fun. Do you meet any famous people? Did you ever meet Tom Selleck?"

"I only wish!" People always seem to think just because I work in films I must know all the stars. Actually, so far I've only played small parts with one or two names you'd recognize, and though they were stars, they were just like anyone else. "Do you know any of

27

the guys on the team?" I ask, hoping to change the subject.

"Oh, sure, all of them," Betsy says. "My boyfriend plays guard. And Jean's boyfriend plays center." She nods at the other girl. "Do *you* know anyone on the team?" she asks with a kind of respectful awe.

"Tom Gordon."

Betsy and Jean exchange surprised glances. "Tom!" Jean exclaims. "Are you going with him?"

"Not really. He just invited me to see him play."

"Isn't Tom going with Marsha?" Betsy asks.

"No, that's Mitch she's going with. Tom used to date Caroline—you know, Caroline Pringle. She's a cheerleader."

For a while the two girls chatter together about different girl-boy combinations, leaving me out. I listen hard because I want to be part of this life, especially if I start to go out with Tom. I wonder who Caroline is and what she looks like and what it is about her that Tom liked, and feel an unpleasant sensation, which must be envy.

Pretty soon the game starts. I lean forward, scanning the players. Tom glances up into the stands for one quick moment and raises a hand, then he takes his position. The other team is already on the floor, and the referee holds the ball up and blows a whistle.

Oh, my, but it's so much more exciting actually seeing the game than reading about it. Everyone is screaming, and the action is so fast, with the ball passing around so much, it's sometimes hard to keep track of where it is. But most of the time my eyes are on Tom. In purple shorts and white shirt, he seems taller than the six two I figured him to be, and he's as graceful as a dancer. It seems as if the ball is always being passed to him.

"Go, Tom!" I scream, forgetting myself. "Come on, Tom!"

The cheerleaders are dancing all over the floor during the half, waving pompoms and chanting slogans about the Rodeo High Rowdies.

Betsy points out the girl Tom used to date, without my asking. "The tall one with the blond hair—that's Caroline." She's pretty and full of bounce.

When the game is finally over, I'm hoarse from all that screaming, and so proud. Our school has won 58–56, and Tom must have scored twenty points. It's such a good feeling—that excitement all around and the noise and the talking and laughing. Betsy and her friend have gone off together and I'm alone again, but I don't feel alone, not like when I came in.

I look at my watch. It's after five and a tremor of fear shoots through me. This is the time I'm normally finishing up with Moffat. What if she calls Mom to find out why I didn't come? I'm such a rotten schemer that it doesn't occur to me until now that I should have phoned Moffat and said I was sick or something.

"You look as though you just lost your best friend," Tom says, appearing in front of me suddenly. His hair is wet and his shirt is damp—it seems he didn't take time to dry himself after his shower. "How'd you like the game?"

My doubts vanish. "It was terrific! You were wonderful!" I'm so full of worshipful admiration that he laughs.

"I only give autographs at halftime." He puts a hand

on my back and propels me down the hall and outside to the parking lot.

"I have to be home by six-thirty," I say. "Where are we going?"

"To eat, because I'm famished, and to talk and get to know each other."

"Great. But six-thirty. I'm serious. My mother's very strict."

He gives me a puzzled look. "I thought it was your job you had to be at."

How easily someone inexperienced at lying can be tripped up. "I go home first. To change."

"And if I don't get you home precisely on time? Do you turn into a pumpkin?"

I clutch my books and stop still. "I think I better go home *now*."

"No, please. I'm sorry I teased you. Of course I'll get you back on time." He opens the car door for me and stands aside.

I'm not sure. I want to see Tom, get to know him, but how? Today is an exception, and to arrange the time I have to deceive. With my schedule and Mom's restrictions maybe the best thing to do is just turn around and go home and forget all about Tom.

"Val?" He's anxious. I can see it in his eyes. And he's not acting; it's for real. He's looking at me with all the insecurity and doubt that I'm feeling.

Oh, Mom, I say to myself, *please understand.* And I climb into his car.

30

Chapter
4

We go to the Wolfburger. Tom says the food here is the best in town. It's a barren place with bare tables and benches, but you can get hungry just smelling the beef broiling over a charcoal fire. We leave our books at a table to hold a place, and go up to order. The counter-man jokes with Tom; he probably comes here a lot.

"What'll you have?" Tom asks. He orders a humon-gous meal—the Double Wolf, large fries, and a giant chocolate shake.

Normally I'd go to the salad bar because I have to keep my weight down. Film makes you look twenty pounds heavier than you really are. But there is no salad bar, and besides, I want everything—the 'burger, the oversize bun, and even the dressing that dribbles down the side, so it's going to be messy to eat.

31

"Single Wolf and a diet cola," I say, figuring I'm compromising with the drink and maybe I'll try *one* of Tom's fries.

"With or without onions?" He eyes me very seriously.

"With."

"Ah," he exclaims, disappointed. "Onions on mine, too, then."

There's something about the way he looks that makes me realize what he means. Maybe I shouldn't have ordered the onions.

We sit down with our food and for a few minutes don't talk. It's been a long time since I've eaten such a wonderfully gooey 'burger, and I savor every bite. Tom, on the other hand, wolfs down his food. "I'm always starved after a game," he says between mouthfuls. He dips one of his fries into some catsup and feeds it to me with a loving look. It's such an intimate sharing, I blush.

"How come I haven't seen you around school before?" he asks. "I'm sure I would have noticed."

For a second I consider telling him the truth, but don't. Even if it's only for a little while, I want to keep this feeling of normalcy. And anyway, if I told him, everything would change. That barrier would come down so fast, we'd be strangers in a second.

"I've been around. I guess you were just too busy to notice." I dab at my mouth with a paper napkin and watch him. I'm thinking about Caroline.

He checks his watch. "We've used up three-quarters of an hour just getting here and eating. I really feel you might turn into a pumpkin or something if I don't get you home by six-thirty. Tell you what. I start work at seven, but I'm done at ten. Will you be through at your job by then? I could pick you up and bring you home and we'd have more time to talk."

"Can't."

"Why?"

Of course, I couldn't tell him the truth. "My mother picks me up."

"Your mother?"

"Yes. We're very close. My parents are divorced, and she only has me. She's kind of overprotective."

"What's she going to do when you graduate and go off to college next year?"

"I'm not sure I will."

"You're kidding. You're such a good student, at least in English. I can't believe you wouldn't go on. What else would you do?"

"Work."

That stops him for a moment, and I realize he's thinking that I might need to work for the money. "You could go to college at night."

College is a subject I don't want to think about. It's too scary. What if I'm accepted back east? How could I go away and leave Mom? Would she even let me go? It's my right to decide for myself, but how could I hurt her like that?

"What about you?" I ask.

"Caltech or Stanford, I hope, out here. Otherwise I've applied at MIT and Brown."

"And if you don't make it?"

"I'll make it. It's mostly a question of which school will give me more money. My parents are in that middle range where we don't qualify for financial aid, but they don't make enough to send three kids through college, especially expensive ones. I've been working to put money aside, but the account doesn't grow very fast."

I think about the money he just spent on me, and feel guilty. "Let me pay for my . . ." I reach for my purse.

He puts a hand over mine. "There's something you don't know. It's on the house. I work here."

"Oh?"

"I get free dinners, and now and then that includes a friend." He grins sheepishly. "I would have told you . . . but—"

"Ah-*ha*," I exclaim just as he did when I joked about the incoming flight from Tokyo. Suddenly we're grinning at each other and giggling, and he takes the hand sticky with dressing and squeezes it.

The hour passes so quickly, and it's just after six-thirty when we start home. Mom might be watching from the window as she sometimes does, and I think of telling Tom to let me off a block from the house. But I decide against that. If I'm to see him again, I want him to come to my house, not meet me in odd places.

"When will I see you again?" Tom asks when he parks, turning to me.

"Monday. In English." I tremble a little because he looks as if he might kiss me."

"That's not what I mean."

"I know . . . " I giggle, then glance out the window to see the house. Mom *is* watching.

"I've got to go!" I gather up my books and purse, my mind already elsewhere. He puts a hand out to restrain me.

"Valerie. What about after school Monday?"

34

"I can't. I'm sorry. I have to work."

"And I have to work in the evening. How about Friday night?"

I hesitate. Friday, Friday; what's planned for Friday? Nothing, I think. But then again, I can never tell what Maurie might cook up. I open the car door, nervous because Mom is watching, and get out. I don't want Tom to think I'm playing coy, or that I don't want to see him; but the truth is, my time isn't my own. I bend down and look in at him through the open window. "Friday may be all right. Can I let you know?"

His eyes brighten. "Sure. That would be super." We gaze at each other for a long beat, a hundred thoughts passing between us, and not a word said. And then I say good-bye and hurry to the door.

Mom opens the door before I put my key in the lock. "Val!" she exclaims. "Where have you been? You weren't at Moffat's! Who was that in the car? How can you go off without letting me know where you are? I was worried to death!"

Something in me turns stubborn. I know she worries. She has every right to, which makes me feel guilty. Up to now I always let Mom know where I was and when to expect me. Except now I want more freedom. I don't want to have to account for my every moment and thought. Now there's Tom, and I want him to myself. I want to go into my room and close the door and lie on my bed and think about what he said and how he looked at me and made me feel. I don't want questions and accusations.

And because I feel guilty about making her worry, I get angry. Instead of answering, I plunk my purse and books down on the hall table and start up the stairs to my room.

"Don't turn your back on me, Valerie Hall! Who do you think you are? You're more and more like your father every day!"

I put my hands over my ears. The blood rushes to my head. "Stop it! Stop it!" I scream, and then I start to cry, and run the rest of the way to my room.

A moment later Mom knocks, then opens the door without waiting for my answer. She comes to sit on my bed, then touches my back and smooths my hair.

"Sweetheart . . . please forgive me. I was horrible. But you can't imagine how worried I got. I imagined all sorts of terrible things—that you were hurt in an accident, kidnapped, molested. I even called the police, but they laughed at me. They said they don't follow up on missing persons until they're gone at least twenty-four hours. They said you were probably with a boy-friend somewhere! Imagine! I told them that was ridiculous. *I know my child!*"

I lie there sobbing, not wanting to hear what she says, but listening anyway with a small part of my mind.

"Sweetheart, please, don't cry anymore. I'm sorry if I frightened you . . . but please try to understand. You're all I've got. I love you so much that if anyone so much as hurt a hair on your head, I'd kill him!"

I know this is true about my mother. I know that she is completely wrapped up in me and practically breathes for me. I know she loves me, and I love her, but it's such a big burden, being so close.

Mother continues to smooth my hair. I can smell her perfume, always Chanel No. 5, and all of a sudden it

36

sickens me. I want her to get off of me, go away, leave me alone!

"Val, darling," she starts again. "When I phoned Moffat and she said you weren't there and she hadn't heard from you, I nearly *died*."

I sit up abruptly, wipe away the tears, and blurt out, "Why, Mom? Didn't you guess I might have gone to the game, like I said I wanted to? Why did you call Moffat? To check on me?"

Mother's eyes widen, and she presses a hand to her chest. "Oh, my . . . oh, my. . . . Do I deserve this?" She shuts her eyes for an instant, and a tear spills out of each corner. Slowly she gets off the bed and walks toward the door.

"Mother?" There's a note of hysteria in my tone. "Is that why you called?"

She twists around, almost losing her balance on those three-inch heels. There is real fury in her eyes now. "You ought to be ashamed of yourself, talking to me like this! Who is it who brought you up, worked nights waitressing so I could be there in the daytime with you? Who sat up when you had croup? Who gave up going out when men asked—and yes ... oh, yes, they did ask—so I could be with you?"

I have heard these stories before, but never in a way meant to make me ashamed for asking something so ridiculous. But I will not let her get to me. I believe, now, that she did indeed phone Moffat just to check. I sit on the bed cross-legged, unwilling to be penitent, and cross my arms over my chest. "You didn't answer my question, Mother!"

She approaches the bed, hands on her hips, eyes burning with indignation. "Yes, I phoned Moffat . . . but not to 'check' on you! I never figured you for a liar. I assumed my Valerie would abide by our decision to forget about this basketball player. No, I didn't phone to 'check.'"

"Then why did you?"

"To tell you that Maurie called."

My heart does a double flip, and my anger dissipates.

"He said you got the part in the *Love Story* series. That two hundred and eighteen girls tried out, but *you* are one of the ones they want. You, Valerie Hall! That's why I phoned!"

The shock hits me hard. It isn't what I expect to hear. "I got the part?" I ask, incredulous.

"You got the part."

"I did? Mom, really?"

Mom nods, smiles hesitantly, and steps toward me.

"I got it! I got it!" I yell, flinging my arms out to embrace the whole world. I jump off the bed and run into Mom's arms. We hug each other as if nothing bad had just happened between us. And we're both laughing and talking at the same time.

Chapter 5

Mom stands behind me as I put on makeup for my date with Josh Metzger. I apply eyeliner carefully, then fill in the lids with green shadow to match my eyes and the full-skirted silk ankle-length dress. Mom is good with hair and has fixed mine in a chignon so that my profile and neck are emphasized, and I look years older than sixteen.

"I wish I didn't have to go . . ."

Mom picks up some small white flowers—stephanotis, I think—and holds them against my hair. "I wonder if I could weave these into the chignon. . . . Why?"

"I don't know." I do, of course. I'd like to be with Tom tonight, anywhere, even just walking along the beach.

"Ninety-nine percent of the girls in America wish they could be in your shoes." Mom picks up some hairpins. "Imagine, a handsome young man taking you to dinner and then to the premiere of a film. How can you not be excited?"

I meet her eyes in the mirror. "It's just business, again, that's why. It's all for my career. It's so calculated . . . I feel like a pawn in a chess game, and I bet he does too."

"Oh, I don't know." Mom picks up my robe and hangs it back in the closet. "Don't sell Josh Metzger short. He's a nice young man, and he'll inherit his father's agency. He's pretty smart, too, if Maurie isn't exaggerating. Graduated from Yale with all kinds of honors."

"What's he doing working in a talent agency, then?"

"What's wrong with working in a talent agency?"

Everything, I think. Talent agents call people "property" and sell them as if they were shoes or dresses. They don't even much care how good their product is, so long as it sells. Talent agents have one subject of conversation—*money*. Which doesn't put them very high on my list of people to admire, though it does on Mom's. But I don't want to start a fuss, so I say, "I guess there's nothing wrong with working in a talent agency, if that's what you want to do."

"Now, be nice to him, Valerie. Don't challenge him the way you're doing me. He can be important to you. Maurie's grooming him to take over some of his accounts—his younger clients . . . like you. . . ."

I stand up. "I'll be nice to him, Mom. Promise." I hold up two fingers in a Girl Scout pledge. "Up to a point."

"Of course."

"But I don't want to make a habit of going out with him just because he might help my career."

40

"Of course, sweetheart." Mom beams at me. "You look gorgeous. Just the right image for the girl who's going to play Andrea in *Love Story!*"

Image, always *image*. Tonight I'm the romantic teen; tomorrow maybe the selfish brat. Will the real Valerie Hall please step forward? I give Mom a quick kiss on the cheek. She's so pleased for me, so happy, as if she's the one going out tonight. I wish she'd live her own life a bit more. If only she had a job that would burn up some of that creative energy she's loaded with, instead of the dull clerical job she does have, things would be better for me. "Mom?" I ask suddenly. "Did you ever consider going to work for Maurie?"

"Of course not! Why would I want to promote anyone except my own daughter? I have my career cut out for me right here, thank you, taking care of you," she replies.

Mom answers the door and brings Josh into the living room where I'm glancing through *Variety*. I stand up to greet him and we give each other a quick "take" as they say in the industry.

He's about six feet tall and nicely built (probably works out regularly at a gym), and I can see Maurie in his dark, intelligent eyes. He looks scholarly with his small beard and mustache—more like a college professor than a Hollywood type.

"Hello, Valerie." He extends a hand and smiles. "Congratulations on the *Love Story* role. Dad's working with the lawyers already. He says he's going to get you a contract that will set you up for life."

He sounds so much like Maurie that I wonder if it comes naturally or if he's affecting his father's style.

"Thank you," I say, momentarily awed by the prospect of my whole life being set up so early in my career.

"Well, we better be going. The reservations are for seven." Josh turns to Mom. "It's nice meeting you, Mrs. Hall. I expect you'll see a lot more of me from now on. Don't worry about Valerie. There's a cast party later, but we shouldn't be back too late."

Mother is charmed. She's so scornful of most Hollywood types. Flaky and self-centered, she calls them. But Josh she loves. He has manners; he calls her *Mrs. Hall*, not Irene, as Maurie does. And he has the proper respect for money.

I could like Josh, I realize with surprise, then remind myself that he's just an escort whose purpose is to show me off so the Metzger Agency will profit. I'll just act as if I'm auditioning for a part. Once I figure out what role I'm supposed to be playing, the evening should run smoothly.

There's a big silver limousine outside, just for the two of us, with a chauffeur standing at attention near the door. It's like the movies and strikes me as so typically Hollywood that I want to laugh.

The chauffeur opens the car door, then stands aside while Josh helps me in and settles beside me. There's a window between us and the chauffeur, and a small bar and telephone. Amazing.

"I know it's overkill," Josh says as the car moves away from the curb. "I'm embarrassed. This is not my style. I wanted to pick you up in my Rabbit, but Dad laughed at me. 'She's going to be a big star,' he said. 'You don't pull up to Mann's Chinese with a star all dressed up in her finest—in your Rabbit.'"

"That's all right," I say, touched by his obvious discomfort. "It's really kind of camp, don't you think?"

His brown eyes crinkle into a genuinely warm smile. "It certainly is."

"Where are we going to dinner, by the way?"

Again Josh's face takes on a pained expression. "I would have liked to take you to the Café Figaro, maybe, or Joe Allen's. Have you been there? But that's not *de rigueur* for this kind of evening. So we have reservations at the Polo Lounge of the Beverly Hills Hotel."

I don't know what *de rigueur* means, but figure it out from what he says. I've been to the Polo Lounge. It's one of Maurie's favorite places. You can usually see other agents and writers and stars at lunch in the Patio Room. It's a good place for making deals. "Yes, I like the Figaro too," I say. "I've been there a couple of times with other actors, and the food is pretty good."

"You know the film we're seeing?"

"Mom told me, but I forget its name."

"The Battle for Star Planet Three."

"Ah-ha," I say in the tone Tom uses, and it brings a smile to my face that has nothing to do with what we're talking about. Josh smiles too.

"I'm glad you're so nice about it. I was afraid, after *Star Planet One* and *Two*, you'd have wanted to skip this sequel. But we represent three actors in the film, so it's important to go to the opening. And besides, Dad thinks you should get a lot of exposure now that you're going into that series." He pauses and gives me a frankly admiring look. "Anyway, it's no hardship spending the evening with someone as beautiful as you." He seems a bit embarrassed by his own words and laughs,

43

so that what sounded sincere and even a bit naive a moment ago may only be typical Hollywood hype, which is all right too. I don't take words like that to heart anyway.

He tells the chauffeur to return around eight-thirty, and we tread a maroon carpet under an awning and enter the hotel lobby.

The Beverly Hills was built in the years of silent movies. It's old by California standards but still classy. Besides the main building with its guest rooms and shops, there are bungalows where celebrities, such as Elizabeth Taylor and Richard Burton, have stayed. The grounds are lush with tropical flowers and plants.

We go directly to the Polo Lounge where the maître d' greets us both warmly *by name*, though I can't understand how he knows mine, unless Josh told him in advance. We're led to a reserved table facing the main dining area, so we can see everyone and be seen.

"Will this be all right, Mr. Metzger?" the waiter asks politely.

"Fine," Josh says, pressing something into his hand. Then he helps me off with my wrap, and we sit down.

Almost immediately the wine steward comes by to take our orders for cocktails. Josh knows that I'm underage, but also that I can pass for twenty-one and probably won't be asked for ID.

"Valerie?"

"Perrier with a twist of lime," I say.

Josh nods and orders a gin and tonic for himself.

When the drinks come, and a platter of cheeses with crackers, we begin to feel more at ease with each other.

"I still can't believe that I got the part!" I say. "It's

such a crazy business. There must have been a dozen others who could easily have done as well or better . . ."

"Don't be so modest," he says. "It's more than luck. You have a lot of talent and charisma." He picks up a menu. "Do you know that before Vivien Leigh got the part of Scarlett in *Gone With the Wind* they auditioned hundreds of women and shot twenty-four hours of film on screen tests?"

"Really?"

"Clark Gable failed his first screen tests because his ears were too big!"

I giggle.

"And when Louis B. Mayer saw Ava Gardner's screen test, he said, 'She can't talk; she can't act; she's terrific!'"

I nibble on a carrot stick, and laugh. "How do you know all that stuff?"

He sits back, a self-satisfied grin on his face, arms stretched around the back of the booth. "Easy. I'm a movie trivia buff. Ask me something."

"Okay. How did Hollywood get its name?"

"Easy. A Mr. and Mrs. Wilcox from Topeka, Kansas, bought land here to raise figs; that was in 1883. Paid a dollar twenty-five an acre. Mrs. Wilcox brought along two pots of English holly and decided to call the place *Holly*-wood." He cocks his head. "Something harder?"

I blush at what comes out of my mouth. "What are the longest and loudest film kisses?"

He's jubilant. "Loudest—between Jack Palance and Shelley Winters in *I Died a Thousand Times*." Without an instant's hesitation he adds, "Longest—in Hitchcock's *Notorious*, between Cary Grant and Ingrid

Bergman. How about the shortest? The sexiest? The most—"

"No . . .no . . . that's enough." I hold up my hand. "For heaven's sake, how does a philosophy major get interested in such . . . uh . . ." I search for a less insulting word than trivia, but Josh isn't insulted.

"You have to remember, Valerie, I've been an agent's son ever since I can remember. My sister and I grew up on Hollywood gossip. We got it at breakfast, lunch, and dinner. We've had some of the most important stars in Hollywood in our home. I used to think that if I could learn as much as my dad knew about the movie industry, if I could 'talk his language,' he'd spend more time with me, so I read everything I could get my hands on about films and stars, before I was ten. But . . ."

A dark look momentarily crosses his animated face, and I have the odd feeling that he's as much tied to his father in his way as I am to Mom.

"Do you really want to be an agent?" I ask softly.

He gives me a penetrating stare, and then his eyes crinkle into a smile. "Do *you* really want to be an actress?"

We gaze at each other for an uncomfortable moment, each not ready to open up to the other in a way we may later regret. And then we are saved. A smiling waiter, pad poised, comes to our table. "Are you ready to order now, sir?" he asks.

Chapter 6

Hollywood Boulevard, near Mann's Chinese Theater, is about as Hollywood as Hollywood gets. The boulevard is lined with shops. The streets are crowded, especially at night, with every human type you'll ever see—panhandlers; drifters; people selling cheap jewelry, toys, and maps to the homes of the stars; punkers in leather pants and vests with hair standing out all over; tourists . . .

And fans of movie stars.

We pull up to the curb near Mann's, behind a Rolls, another chauffeur-driven limo, and a couple of Mercedes-Benzes. A big floodlight pierces the night sky. Curiosity seekers peek into the cars, pushing and gesturing. I draw back, scared by the press of strange faces. Two policemen on horseback start ordering the crowd back, so there's a narrow lane for people to walk by.

It's the first time I've been to a premiere, and I'm as nervous as I was the first time I ever auditioned.

"It's a zoo," Josh says before we get out of the car. "And we're the animals. But you might as well get used to it. It comes with the territory."

The chauffeur jumps out of the car, right in front of the entrance. He opens the door for us and steps aside. Josh gets out and reaches a hand in for me.

There's a wide lane leading into the theater, cordoned off on both sides by ropes that hold back the crowds. I flinch at the sudden roar; at the press of bodies against the ropes, hands reaching out to touch me; at the bright lights flashing.

"Is that the star? Who's he?"

Hands stretch across the barrier, thrusting pads and pencils at me. "Autograph this for my sister? Autograph! Autograph!" Papers of all sizes and shapes bloom in front of me.

"Go ahead," Josh whispers. "And *smile*. They won't hurt you."

I scribble my name on five or six papers, looking into the strange, overexcited faces of people who don't really know who I am. A photographer comes toward us, and flashbulbs pop. And then behind us another car pulls up, and the crowd's attention shifts as quickly as a school of fish startled by a shark. A scream goes up, and voices rise at the sight of a real celebrity.

Josh tucks my arm through his and whispers, "Next year, this time, your name and face will be as familiar as Teri Garr's."

I laugh. *"How?"*

"Just leave it to me."

I'm too wired to wonder what it might be like, but this small taste of fame is not entirely unpleasant.

The theater lobby is aglitter with show people, and agents, and people involved in the making of the film, and their relatives and hangers-on. Everyone is dressed up, the men in tuxedos and the women in elegant dresses. Everyone is watching everyone else, trying to see who's important.

The walls scream with garish pictures of the characters in *Star Planet III*, and above the din of ordinary conversation comes the music from the film. I try to appear natural, as if I belong, but I don't recognize many faces and I feel so very very young.

Josh leads me through the crowds deftly, a hand at my elbow, stopping now and then to introduce me to this producer, or that well-known director. They are names to me, and it's hard to make small talk, not that it matters, because as soon as an introduction is over, they turn to someone else.

Everywhere I hear words like "agent . . . contracts . . . biggest deal . . . option . . . a million dollars." Heady stuff.

Maurie is holding court near the bar, a beautiful redhead at his side. She holds a glass of white wine and smiles at everyone, maybe because Maurie's attention is on the two men who are talking "deals." I wonder if she's important to him, his girlfriend, or if, like Josh, he's just her escort for the night.

"Valerie, darling." Maurie puts an arm around my waist. "I'd like you to meet some people . . ." and he introduces me to the men, who are both independent producers. The young woman brightens at the sight of Josh.

According to Maurie, I'm the next big box-office draw. In industry-speak that means people will see any movie I'm in just because of my name. In Hollywood that means lots of money. I smile agreeably, but it doesn't go to my head. Maurie hypes all of his clients this way.

It's not long before we're forgotten, and Josh moves me on to meet others. Finally the house lights flicker, and we go inside to our seats.

It's the typical sequel sci-fi, with lots of special effects and odd-shaped creatures and a cast of humans dressed in Hollywood's version of twenty-first-century gear. In some ways it's as good as *Star Planet I* and maybe even better than *Star Planet II*.

In most theaters people start filing out when the final credits hit the screen. But not at a premiere. Everybody stays to the very last. Josh whispers that they're looking for their names, or the names of people they know, on the screen, looking for whom to put the blame on if it's a bad picture, or whom to envy if it's good.

"Do you want to join Maurie and his crowd?" Josh asks afterward. "They're going to the Perinos."

"Do you?"

He hesitates. "Dad would like us to be there, but to tell the truth, I'd rather not."

"Then let's don't!"

"Do you want to go home?" Before I can answer, he adds, "Or would you like to see what I sold my soul to the Devil for?"

Intrigued, I opt, naturally, for the second choice. Without a word he hustles us out of the theater, waves at his father from a distance but doesn't stop to explain, and gets us into the limo before Maurie can put pressure on us to come to his after-theater party.

"Take the Santa Monica west," he tells the chauffeur as the car pulls out into traffic. Josh leans back, yanks off his bow tie, undoes the top button of his shirt, and sighs like someone who has just been freed from bondage.

"Where are we going?" I ask, but he won't say and instead turns the conversation to a discussion of the film we just saw.

Before I know it we're in Marina del Rey, pulling into a big parking lot. Ahead of us is a low building, the Marina Yacht Club. He tells the chauffeur to wait, then takes my hand and, with long strides, leads me through the parking lot, along a narrow walk, down some well-lit steps, to a dock and the boat slips.

"There," he says, pointing proudly.

Before us is a beautiful sailboat with *Pirate's Treasure* printed in Gothic letters on the bow. "A thirty-six-footer," he explains proudly. The white hull is immaculate. Every inch of it seems to have been scrubbed and polished at least three times.

"Come on, I'll show you." Almost breathless with excitement, he leaps from the dock to the deck and extends a hand to me. I slip out of my heels and jump the short distance, almost falling into his arms.

He loves the boat. He touches everything—the smooth wood, the dials, the wheel. He shows me the cabin, which is small but compact and has a space for sleeping, a refrigerator, a tiny stove, and cabinets to

51

hold provisions and dishes. Then he takes a couple of colas from the fridge and some plastic cups, and we return to the deck where he sets up a small table and puts out some chips. It's getting cold, and I wrap my shawl tight around me. Josh is so hot with excitement, he doesn't notice.

"Isn't this *something?*" he asks.

"Oh, yes!" The water laps quietly against the side of the boat. Sea gulls cry far off, and a buoy sounds out in the channel. Lights on nearby boats give the place a magical feeling. It's as if, at any moment, music will play and people will be walking about and the scene will spring to life.

He nods. "Graduation present, with a string attached: that I come home to work at the agency."

"*That's* what you meant about selling your soul! But what else would you have liked to do?"

Josh hunches forward, hands squeezed between his knees. "Don't laugh." He glances quickly at me, then away. "I'd have liked to teach philosophy in a college. But you don't make a living doing that without a doctorate degree, and then barely."

"So? What's stopping you?"

"It would mean six more years of college . . . and having to depend on my father to support me. As you can guess, I also like the things money can buy." He gestures around him.

"Then you have what you want."

"Not exactly, but life is a series of compromises, isn't it?"

There's an odd silence between us, and I ask, "Do you like being an agent?"

Josh moves so his face falls into the shadows. "I'm not sure yet. Do you like being an actress?"

"Yes, but I've never had the chance to be anything else."

"Well, there you are. Life is full of decisions made for you by circumstance or by others."

"I don't think so. I think others may try to influence us, or circumstances may push us into choosing certain paths, but the final choice is our own."

"Life is a series of compromises," Josh says again. "You'll know what I mean when you have some important decision of your own to make."

"What do you think of Josh?" Mom asks the next day.

I notice she has not asked me what I think of Tom, not asked me what Tom and I did together Friday. Naturally. Now that I have the TV role she figures there's no future in *that* relationship. It will die of malnutrition. If the pilot sells and we go into production on a regular basis, we'll do an episode a week. My schoolwork will be done at the studio; seeing Tom will be almost impossible.

We are sitting on the patio. My work these last few years has paid well enough for us to afford a modest home in the San Fernando Valley. The pretty flagstone patio off the living room looks out at a wall of scarlet bougainvillaea.

Mom sits at the glass-topped patio table, thumbing through her stamp collection. Everyone we know saves foreign stamps for her, and once a month she examines them with a magnifying glass, reads up on the country, or the flower or animal or person depicted, then, with a sigh of longing, hinges the stamps in her book. She has a positive lust to travel, and someday, when I've made more money, I'm going to surprise her with a trip to Europe.

"What do you think?" Mom asks again, looking up, because I haven't answered. I'm absorbed in the book reviews of the Sunday *Los Angeles Times*.

"About Josh?" I stop to think. "He's different from what I expected. Kind of nice. But weak."

"Oh?"

"Yes. I think so. For one thing, he's always quoting Maurie. I get the feeling he cares too much about what his father thinks."

Mom gives me a funny look.

"He'd like to be a college professor—of philosophy—but he's been, er, *seduced* . . . by what money can buy."

"There's nothing wrong with *money*," Mom says.

"No." I try to go back to what I was reading. Mom holds a magnifying glass to a stamp.

"Money is what makes the world go round."

"Oh, *Mother!*"

"Don't 'Oh, Mother' me. When your father left, all I had was a hundred and seventy-two dollars, an eleven-year-old car, and you. How do you think I felt?"

"We did all right."

"Yes, and we'll do even better." Mom cuts the end of an opaque envelope and, with a tweezer, removes a stamp. "It's going to be better for you, not like it was for me. You're going to be able to *choose*, to do what you like. That's why it's so important to listen to Maurie."

I shrug.

"Listen to me, Val. Look at me!"

54

I look up. Mom's eyes are bright. I sometimes think *she* should have gone into acting; her face is so expressive.

"Maurie Metzger is one smart man. I know what you think of him. I know you think he's crass and insensitive and just out for the most bucks, but you're wrong. He believes in his clients, and he'll fight to get the best for them. And he loves that son of his. If he thinks Josh would do well in the agency, he's probably right. Maybe he knows his son hasn't the staying power to go through six more years of school. Maybe he knows Josh likes good things . . . the things money can buy. And maybe, too, he wants Josh there beside him, to hand over the business to one day. Is that so awful?"

"Why are you so angry about this, Mom?"

She pauses, and all the fire in her eyes subsides. She smiles at me, a little embarrassed. "I don't really know. Maybe because you called Josh weak. Just because he likes money—"

"You like money too. So do I. But I don't think of *you* as weak."

Mother gives a little shrug. She is annoyed. "It's just that . . . I hoped—I hoped you'd *really* like him."

Mother watches me for a reaction, but I have none to give. Josh is nice, but he's eight or ten years older than I. He's kind and thoughtful, but he cares too much for money. But besides all that, it's a question of chemistry. Josh doesn't make me feel all soft inside, the way Tom does.

"Mom." There must be something tentative in my voice because she's on guard almost immediately. "I want to skip some of my afternoon classes and go to school things. Just until we get into production," I add hurriedly. "Maybe I'll try out for cheerleader. Join the school paper. Oh, I don't know. I just want to be normal for a while."

An odd smile crosses Mom's face. "It's this boy, the basketball player, isn't it?"

My face burns. "Tom. Yes."

Mother shakes her head a little. "Well . . . I don't know. I guess it can't do much harm . . ."

I hold my breath. "You mean you don't mind?"

Mother raises an eyebrow. "You've worked very hard these last years. And when you start the series. . . . Sure . . . why not."

Chapter 7

I meet Tom for lunch almost every day now. Before, I'd eat yogurt on the run, reading my assignments while spooning it down. But now I sit with him, and sometimes with Betsy, Jean, and their boyfriends, or go across to the fast-food stands with them. We gorge on tacos, 'burgers, and fries. If Mom knew, she'd explode. "Think what it will do to your skin! The calories in that fried junk!"

But it can't be doing all that much harm. Last week she looked me over and said, "You're absolutely blooming. I guess we *were* working you too hard."

Tom thinks I've quit my job and figures I'll be working again soon, so we had better spend every free minute together. And we do.

Last Saturday we went hiking in Malibu Canyon. The fog hangs like a gray gauze over the trail most of the way, and even our voices seem muted. A rabbit bounds right across our path, startling a covey of quail who take to the sky with a mad flutter of wings. Delighted, I laugh, and Tom squeezes my hand. He knows so much about things I never learned—the names and songs of different birds, all the plants and trees. And each time I exclaim at some new thing, he's as pleased as if he just won an Emmy.

About noon the sun burns holes in the fog until it grows thin and wispy and just floats away, leaving us a bright, sparkling world hung with dew. We find a high clearing and put down our lunch things, then amble to the edge of the plateau.

"I feel as though we're the only people left in the world," I say.

Tom tightens a hand around my waist. "I feel . . . very happy . . ."

Far below, the sun glints off the sea, and small boats, their white sails plump with wind, skip along the surface.

"Have you ever sailed?" I ask Tom, thinking of Josh's boat and wondering if he is out on the water today.

"On lakes, not the ocean," Tom says. "My family likes to vacation in the Sierras. We backpack, all five of us. Hike all day, then camp by some alpine meadow or lake. My brothers and I always take a swim to wash off the trail dust . . . and the waters are pure ice. It's beautiful up there, away from everything. We catch trout for breakfast, and Mom fries it in bacon. You can't imagine the smell, and the taste! Mmm."

"I never did things like that."

"What were your summers like?"

"Fun, in different ways from yours. We never left the city. Mom would get two weeks off, and we'd bus to the beach and spend the day there, and then we'd eat out. I guess I'm a city person. I love the smell of auto exhaust and the noise of the streets and the people. When Mother and I—" I stop because I almost tell how Mom taught me, even when I was very young, to study the way people reveal themselves. "Look," she'd say as we lay together on a beach towel, "that old woman. Watch how she trudges through the sand, kind of hunched over, those skinny legs splayed out for balance. See that pretty girl over there? Notice how she swings her hair back and forth to get that boy's attention, and that little boy, how his face gets all bent out of shape when he's angry."

Tom picks up the unfinished sentence. "Mother and I . . . what?"

"Oh, nothing," I say brightly. "Let's eat. I'm starved."

He gives me a puzzled glance, and we go back to the blankets and lay out the food. Tom pours the fruit drinks, and I take out thick chicken sandwiches stuffed with Swiss cheese, tomatoes, and sprouts. I made them in the morning while Mother watched. She sang tunelessly, conveying to me, without a word spoken, how hurt and abandoned she felt.

"You know," Tom says after a while. "Sometimes I feel like you've got a big secret life, apart from what anyone sees, that you don't talk about."

A shiver of fear runs through me. For a second I wonder if Betsy or Jean or someone else has said anything. I think, too, of those first awkward days when it was so hard to find things to talk about. What, after all, have we in common when so much of my life can't be shared? For a second I wonder if I dare tell him about my work. Surely he'd understand. But no. I don't dare take the chance. It could change everything good between us.

"What kind of secrets do you think I keep?" I am lying on the ground, hands under my head. A squirrel jumps from a tree branch to the trunk and watches us. Tom leans over me.

"Well . . ." With one finger he traces my eyebrows, sending tingles down my arms and legs. "You're so mysterious. Before you quit working, you were like a ghost at school—there but not there, a loner. I asked some of the guys if they knew anything about you. They didn't think you dated. You didn't belong to any of the school clubs. You didn't seem to have any special friends; and you were always running off as soon as your last class ended. *Do* you have a secret life, Valerie Hall?"

Tentatively I reach a hand up to touch his face, and close my eyes at the warmth of his skin. In all the times I've acted love scenes I was always conscious of camera angles and where noses fit and keeping the right expression on my face whether or not I liked the boy I was kissing. But I never felt like this—all expectant and shivery and wanting.

"Do you have a secret life, Valerie?" Tom asks again, whispering.

I shake my head very slightly, not opening my eyes, expectant. And in the next moment I feel his lips on mine, soft and sweet. Oh, so sweet. Without thinking, I reach my arms up to bring him close. Without thinking, I give him back kiss for kiss. And when he lifts his face and I open my eyes, tears are running down my cheeks.

In the month Maurie and Josh are negotiating the contract and the producer is ironing out the production details, I can almost believe life will always be this way. When Suzie phones, our talk is already of two different worlds.

"I tried out for this part in a Universal movie," she says. Or, "You know the part I auditioned for last month in that toothpaste commercial?"

And I—free from the three phone calls a day to Maurie now that my future is lined up, free from acting and singing classes—go on and on about Tom. "He's so wonderful, Suzie! Mails me these funny, funny cards. Sent me a card with a heart on it, and inside he wrote, 'Lub Dub . . . Lub Dub.' You know, heart sounds? Then instead of 'Lub Dub' he writes 'Lub-Val.' Get it?"

"You *are* hooked!" Suzie says. "What's going to happen when you start working? You haven't told him yet?"

I hesitate and take a deep, scared breath. "Not yet."

"What are you waiting for?"

"I can't, Suzie! I've waited so long, that I couldn't now, even if I wanted to. He'd say I lied to him. Our worlds are so different when I'm working. I don't even want to *think* about what happens if the pilot succeeds and we go ahead with the series."

"It's your life, Val . . . but if it were me . . ."

Maybe Suzie is right. In the meantime a stubborn part of me doesn't want to think about anything except how wonderful it is to get up each morning and go to school, how special each day is because I'm in love.

"Maurie called today," Mom announces when I get home from school one day. "He wants us in his office at three tomorrow to sign the contracts." There is a glint of relief in Mom's eyes, as if now, at last, life will return to normal.

I tell Tom on Friday that I can't see him after school because I have to go somewhere.

"A job interview?"

"Umm," I say. "Something like that." His puzzled look is back, and I change the subject.

Already there's a distancing taking place in my head. Although my heart feels as heavy as a bowling ball, I know that what's between us has to be over soon. Tom takes my withdrawal for fear. "Don't worry, Val. You'll get the job, whatever it is. And we'll get together after the game Friday night. You're coming, of course."

"Of course."

But I haven't figured on Maurie, my mother, and Josh.

Mom really dresses up for the contract-signing occasion. She's stylish and elegant in a new pink linen suit, off-white silk blouse, and matching purse and pumps. She's done her chestnut-colored hair to add another two inches of height.

Despite her protests I wear the same jeans and white sweater I intend to wear to the basketball game tonight. Why should it matter? All I have to do is sign my name and leave.

But as soon as we enter Maurie's office it's clear there's more to this than I imagined. Norma greets Mom with a big hug and me with a huge smile and a bouquet of flowers, compliments of the producer. She knocks on the door to Maurie's office, peeps in, and says, "They're here!" then holds the door wide for us.

"Sweetheart!" Maurie, a bright, toothy grin on his

tanned face, bounds across the thick carpeting to greet us halfway.

Josh appears subdued, almost as if we have interrupted an argument between him and his father.

"Irene!" Maurie exclaims, putting an arm around my mother. "You're absolutely radiant. No wonder you have such a gorgeous daughter." He leads us to the plum-colored suede sofa, then goes to sit on the edge of his enormous desk. "This is a real occasion!" He picks up a cigar and rolls it between his fingers. "First, congratulations are in order for our girl. Then I'll go over the contract details, and you are going to be very, very pleased. Then . . ." He draws out the last word. "Then, the four of us are going to have dinner at . . . Ma Maison."

Mother cries out and claps her hands together like a delighted child.

I say, "I *can't!* I have an appointment tonight."

"Oh, pish-posh!" Mother cries. "What's a silly basketball game at a time like this?"

"Mother! You knew . . ."

"Break your date, sweetheart," Maurie says. "You can't disappoint your mother or me. Or Josh either, for that matter. Isn't that right, Josh?"

"Right," Josh says without enthusiasm from across the room.

"But—but I'm not dressed for a fancy restaurant!"

"Pish-posh," Mom says. "We'll stop by the house, and you can change in five minutes."

I look from Mom to Maurie. There's no question in their faces as to what they expect of me. "*You* go, without me!" I cry, out of excuses.

"How can we do that? It's *your* celebration, sweetheart. Now stop making a fuss. How can you disappoint your wonderful mother?" Maurie asks.

Josh looks at me and our eyes meet briefly. He must see how upset I am, but he remains distant.

"Here's to a beautiful, bright, and talented young lady . . . and to her charming mother."

Mom blushes. "And thanks to the man who made it all possible, and to his brilliant son, Josh."

"Beginnings. That's what we're cheering," says Maurie. "Valerie's career. My new partnership with Josh. How about that!" says Maurie.

"I don't know what you did to them at that audition, Valerie, sweetheart," Maurie says, "but they're real hot for you. Real hot. And I've got a dandy contract to prove it." He picks up a thick sheaf of papers and waves it at us.

I cringe a little at Maurie's crude compliment, but Mom giggles. "Didn't I tell you to think positive, honey? Didn't I tell you when you went for that audition that you'd get the part?"

Mom tells me that every audition I try out for.

"Nobody believes in me the way you do," I say to her. "Maurie, may I use a phone?"

"Sure, sweetheart." He waves at the phone on his desk.

How can I speak to Tom with everyone listening?

Josh gets up. "She can use the phone in my office."

As we leave the room I hear Maurie say, "Valerie's right about you, Irene. I've always admired your faith in her, the way you buoyed her up when she lost hope. That's what good parenting is all about. Now, Josh . . .

he's the best and the brightest and . . ." Josh grimaces as he opens the door to his office.

Chapter 8

"Sign here, Valerie," Maurie says, offering me a pen. "And, Irene, you sign just below, since Val's a minor."

For an hour we have been listening to Josh explain the contract details. He cuts through the legal jargon like an attorney and goes straight to the heart of things, and I think he would make a good college professor.

Mom sits, hands tightly folded, every cell in her body attentive. Now and again she asks a question. Maurie says she's got a real sharp business sense.

It *is* a great contract. I will be paid almost a million dollars over three years if the pilot gets network approval, they like *me*, and the series is made; and every time an episode is repeated or shown in some foreign country, I get more. Also there are products I can endorse. And after three years they renegotiate.

"By this time next year you'll be on the cover of *TV Guide*. You won't be able to walk down Rodeo Drive without being besieged for autographs," Maurie says.

It's mind-boggling. I can't believe people would pay me so much for what I enjoy.

"You do realize," Josh says in a voice that catches everyone's attention, "that this is a *three-year commitment*, that you are tying yourself up for three—"

Maurie's smile vanishes. "*Josh*. Check if Norma is still outside, will you?"

Josh ignores Maurie. He's sitting on the edge of his father's desk, arms firmly crossed over his chest. More softly he says, "Valerie, you do realize what this means, don't you?"

"Of *course* she realizes what it means!" Mom says. "It means three years of steady work instead of worrying each day when the next job will come through, instead of going to endless auditions! It's a chance to grow, to become a mature actress!"

Josh ignores her. "Once you sign this contract you're *in*, Valerie. Assuming the pilot goes, and they like you, you'll be expected to do six episodes, then more probably. You can't decide in two months, or four or five, that you'd rather be doing something else."

"Josh! *Enough!*" Maurie cries. "What are you trying to do?"

"Valerie knows what a commitment is," Mom says. "Go ahead, darling, sign!"

I look from one to the other of them. "I don't know . . ."

"What do you mean, you *don't know?*" Maurie bellows. "You came to me two years ago asking that I make you a star. I work my tail off getting you show-case roles, planting your name in the right places, getting out news to the trade papers about you . . . priming you for this moment. Well, you've made it now. You've arrived. This is what you and I and your mother worked for. For this day. And you 'don't know'?"

I feel like squirming into a hole, away from all those eyes boring into me.

"Maurie . . . don't . . ." Mom admonishes, putting a hand on his arm. She turns to me. "Valerie, darling. Everything Maurie says is true. What don't you know? Is there something you don't understand?"

"I may want to go to college," I say, looking down at my hands. "I may even want to go . . . back east."

From the look on Mother's face, my words really hit below the belt. East means Daddy.

"You can *always* go to college," Maurie says. "You're young. College will be there, whenever. A career like this doesn't wait."

"You can't take a four-year break *now!*" Mother's face flushes. "In four years you'll be back to square one. Nobody will remember you! You'll have to start all over again!"

"What's such a big deal about college anyway?" Maurie asks. "You'll learn more about people, about life, *doing it* right here than you'll ever learn from books!"

A small cynical smile crosses Josh's face.

"This is ridiculous," Mom says. "Don't make me crazy, Valerie. Sign it! Sign it so we can get out of here tonight and go celebrate, like Maurie said."

Am I making a big thing out of nothing? I don't even know right now. Everything they say is true. Maurie worked hard to get me to this point. *I* worked hard.

Isn't this what I've wanted to do with my life ever since I could walk? How can I even consider turning down such a marvelous contract to live as an ordinary college coed? I look to Josh for support, for an answer, but he's gazing up at the ceiling.

I'm all mixed up. Do I want acting for myself or for Mom? Do I want college *to learn* or to get away from Mom? What should I *do*?

Mom picks up the pen and puts it back in my hand. "Sign, honey. You won't be sorry. This is the day we've all been working for. Trust me."

I stare at the line on the contract where my name is typed, and the letters blur. I'm trapped. I've gone too far with this to back down now. Mom's probably right; she usually is. I pull at the neck of my sweater; I'm suffocating. And I sign.

When we reach home, there's a message on the answering machine. "Val? This is Tom. Thought we had a date. What happened? You okay?"

I wind the tape back and listen again, and again, just to hear his voice, but it doesn't ease the growing ache. When I phoned him from Josh's office, no one answered, and now there's no way to reach him until Sunday night when he gets back from a soccer meet in San Diego.

"You could go sailing with Josh Sunday," Mom says, watching me. "I thought it was very nice of him to ask. As long as Tom's away, what difference—"

"Stop pushing me at Josh!"

"I'm not pushing! Do as you please. Why should I care? But if I were you, I sure wouldn't sit around brooding all weekend while my boyfriend's out having himself a good time."

"I don't want to be with Josh! Don't you understand? I want to be with Tom!"

Mom shrugs. "Do as you please. Josh was only being nice. At least you'll be out in the fresh air . . ."

Away from you, I feel like screaming.

And when Josh does phone later, I accept, but for just that reason.

I wish for rain or fierce winds, even an earthquake, so I can stay home, but Sunday dawns a perfect blue-sky day, warm but not hot, with the gentlest of breezes.

Josh rings the bell right on time. He's wearing a dark blue shirt and white shorts that show his strong, hairy legs. Mom would like him to come in, but he declines. I get the feeling he has no desire to spend even a minute making small talk with her, and soon we're on our way.

"You really didn't have to ask me, you know, just because you're my agent now," I say on the way to the marina.

"You think that's why I asked?" He looks sideways at me in surprise.

"Well, wasn't it?"

"I never do anything I don't want to."

"Oh?"

"Oh, what?"

"I always seem to do things I don't want to."

"Like what?"

"Like trying to please Mom or Maurie, and others, instead of myself."

"I thought so." He chuckles. "You didn't want to come. Your Mom insisted, right? And you haven't

70

learned to say no. That's just what I mean when I talk about how we don't always make decisions for ourselves." He glances my way. "That's okay. I'll take you home."

"No, no. Don't. It's *okay!*"

"Make up your mind, Val. You can't go on pleasing the whole darn world and still do what you want." He makes a U-turn. "We're going back."

"Josh, wait. It's such a beautiful day and I've never been sailing, and if I go home, I'll have to face Mom. It's just that Mother and Maurie seem to be using me, using *us*. I even think they're trying to pair us up. . . ."

He pulls the car to the curb and cuts the engine, then turns to me. "In this business you have to get used to the fact that you're going to be used. The best thing you can do is see that you're well used. I know what my father's up to, but I can play that game too. Why should we let your mother and my father turn us against each other just because we know they're manipulating? Look, Val, I like you. You're honest, sweet, a good companion. Let's be friends. If you like sailing, well, we can go out again together. Maybe I'll teach you how to handle the boat so we can compete in some of the yachting events. In any case, it will get you away from your mother, which is something I think you very much want. It'll give you a chance to meet other kinds of people, not just actors . . . some of my friends, for instance. I have no ulterior motives . . . no romantic intentions. Understand?"

What he says makes sense, and the tension begins to ebb. Smiling, I say, "Thanks."

"Shake." He holds out a hand, a strong, artistic hand

with long fingers, and we shake, and then he starts the car again. "Now, let's go sailing and have us a good time."

When we reach the marina, Josh loads me down with bags of groceries and extra jackets. "You're really interested in me for my packhorse abilities," I joke, and stagger across the parking lot as if I'm carrying an elephant. He laughs; we're totally at ease with each other now.

His friends Dave and Erin are waiting at the boat. They have already uncovered the sails and stowed the covers below deck. Dave, wearing a tattered Yale T-shirt, is a tall, loose-limbed man with a terrier's soulful eyes. He leaps to the dock and relieves me of my packages, making cracks about Josh who, he says, always takes advantage of the opposite sex. Erin, slender and redheaded, holds out a hand to help me climb aboard.

It is a time of busyness, of stowing gear and groceries and exchanging news and jokes, of turning on switches and untying lines; and finally, engine on, we glide slowly out of the slip into the harbor.

Moving out to sea takes all of Josh's attention. His eyes are everywhere, but he looks as if he's in total harmony with the world.

It's all so new and exciting. The air smells salty; gulls shriek overhead. Music floats up from below, and every boat that passes we wave or call out to. When we pass the breakers, Dave unties some straps and hoists sail. Then, motor off, we go skimming almost silently over the waves, and I think how really perfect it would be if Tom were here too.

For a while I sit there hugging my knees, gazing at the shoreline or the sea, enjoying the slap of wind against my face. Erin is below looking for drinks, and Dave is sunning himself on the aft deck.

"Take over," Josh says from the helm.

"Me? Oh, no! I'd sink us!"

"Come on. It's easy. All you have to do is keep the needle in the middle."

Erin appears with a trayload of goodies just as I take my place behind the wheel, and Dave reaches a lazy hand down for a cola.

It's harder to steer than I expect. The boat pulls to the right or left, and I struggle to keep it on course, but Josh encourages me and soon I get the knack of it. Relaxed, I recite, "I must go down to the sea again," in a deep, dramatic voice.

Erin immediately says, "One if by land, and two if by sea."

Dave calls out, "The sun was shining on the sea."

And Josh supplies, "Home is the sailor, home from the sea."

For the next five minutes they toss out quotations about the sea so fast, I am overwhelmed. Awed by their intellect, I turn mute. I search my memory for something, anything, to offer. Finally I shout, "From sea to shining sea!"

They laugh.

"Bobby Shaftoe's gone to sea!"

A look, a smile; they accept me and I feel so good! They are different from the kids I know in the industry; I want to be like them.

Chapter 9

Tom calls Sunday night. "I tried to reach you Friday, Val. Where were you?"

"I tried to reach you, too, to say I couldn't get to the game, but there was no answer."

"What happened?"

"I . . . had to go to dinner with friends of my mother's. There was no getting out of it. We didn't get back until late." I take a breath. "How was the game, and the San Diego trip?"

He goes on excitedly about the basketball game Friday night and how disappointed he was afterward when he couldn't celebrate the win with me. He tells me in detail about the ride to San Diego and the game there, and then about the fun the team had at Lion Country before they drove back.

I listen with all my senses, and wish I could be beside him now, holding his hand, seeing the excitement in his eyes.

"What did *you* do Sunday, besides miss me?" he asks at last.

"Went sailing."

"Really? Who with?"

"Some people. You wouldn't know them."

There was a pause as if he's digesting this incomplete information, and then he asks in a somewhat altered voice, "Have fun?"

"Yes, as a matter of fact. It was different, and exciting, and the people I was with were very . . . interesting."

I know he expects me to say more . . . something about the people; but I think he would not really want to know that I was out with Josh, so I remain silent.

"Did you hear from Stanford or Caltech yet?" I ask brightly when the silence goes on a beat too long.

"Not yet. The letters should be coming next week. Some of the kids have already gotten theirs. You?"

I hesitate, thinking how months ago I applied to Cornell, Reed, and UCLA with so much hope, and now it looks as if my future is settled. "Not yet."

"I really hope you get into Cornell. I know what it means to you—looking up your father, getting to know him. After all, you are half his genes too."

The reminder, like a probe, strikes something deep, and for a moment it's hard to breathe. I say, "I don't even know where he lives, Tom." Sometimes Maurie says, when I ask, that he's playing off-Broadway in a Shakespeare play, or in Hartford, doing Ibsen . . .

"Does he ever write?"

"I don't think so. Not anymore, anyway, if he ever did. Mom never says, and if he wrote, I doubt she'd ever let me see the letter."

75

"That's sad. Just because she hates him, you shouldn't have to be deprived."

His words touch me. "Could you come over?" I ask in a small voice. "I need you."

There's only a slight pause, then he says, "Be by in ten minutes."

When his car pulls up, I grab my jacket and tell Mom I'll be back in an hour. "But it's so late!" she objects. "And it's raining cats and dogs!"

"I didn't see him Friday night, remember?"

Mom is about to answer when the bell rings. I open the door, grab Tom's hand, and run through the rain to his car. We get in and, without a word, reach for each other. He takes me in his arms, and I want to stay that way with the sound of rain on the roof and the windshield wipers swishing their comforting sound and the sense that everything's okay now.

"Where shall we go?"

"Anywhere. To the end of the rainbow. To a distant planet. Anywhere, just so we're together." I move as close to Tom as I can, and lean my head against his shoulder. He holds the wheel with one hand, and my hand with the other.

I guess it's the darkness of the night, the feeling that we're enclosed in a cocoon, that makes me say things I haven't even admitted to myself.

"I miss my father. I hardly remember him, but I miss him."

Tom nods.

"Sometimes I imagine walking down a street and there's this man coming toward me. I get terribly excited. Without knowing how, I know it's my father. I start crying and call, 'Daddy, Daddy!' And . . . Isn't it silly?" We are driving through the rainy streets, and everything blurs, the street lamps, the lights of oncoming cars."

"No, it's not silly. Maybe you're more like him than you are like your mother. You should have the chance to meet and find out."

"How? I've thought of tracking him down, but Mom would be furious." I pause, thinking about that. "Sometimes I hate her. Is that too awful to say?"

"Everyone dislikes his mother at some time or another."

"But *hate?* How can I both love her and hate her? She's been mother *and* father to me. She's sacrificed so much that I owe her everything. I'm so much in debt, I'll never pay her back!"

"Parents don't expect repayment. They do what they do out of love."

His words pass me by. "I feel stifled!" I cry. "I can't figure out anymore if I want something because I really want it, or because I'm talked into wanting it."

"What things?"

"Things."

"There you go getting secretive again." Tom releases my hand and tries to read my face in the dark.

I swallow a sharp lump in my throat. If ever there's a time to tell him about my acting, it's now. Next week I start work on the pilot. How will I explain two weeks away from school? I'll be working all day, taking lessons on the set and studying my lines for the next day in the evenings. But I could see Tom on weekends!

Tell him, part of me urges. *You can't keep it secret for-*

ever. With each falsehood you're in deeper. He'll have to know eventually.

But *not now*. He'll start treating me different, become self-conscious, maybe be threatened by the people I know. And, after all, it's only two weeks, then I go back to school as if nothing has happened. There'll be months before the networks decide whether to finance the series. By then it will be late summer, and everything may be different. No. Just a little longer. *Maybe Saturday.*

The week passes all too soon. Every day I savor its moments—sitting at lunch with Tom and our friends; drinking in the sharing and laughter, the sense of belonging. They tease me. "Tom's never liked any girl longer than a week. What's with you two, anyway?" I laugh, so pleased to feel normal, and loved. I tingle with pleasure, as Tom walks me from class to class, a hand on my shoulder, or around my waist. I think of no one else. Even Mom's tight-lipped silence can't spoil things.

And then, too soon, it's Saturday night, the last chance to be with Tom before I start work. All day my stomach has been knotted with fear. I still haven't invented the best explanation. "I'm going to visit an aunt in Utah for two weeks? My mother's sick? I have a chance to visit New York?" None of these excuses sound genuine or believable. I *must* tell him the truth!

Something is wrong from the start. When Tom comes to call for me, there's something different about him—a stiffness, a remoteness that I've never known before. He's polite enough to Mom, but when he looks at me, there's a blankness in his eyes that sends shivers down my arms and legs and turns me clammy. I try to cover up with jokes about his car. "Last week it was a flat tire. I helped put on the spare," I quip to Mom. "The week before, it was a clogged fuel line, and I had to steer while Tom pushed. He's training me to be an auto mechanic!"

Mom smiles. Tom does not.

My heart begins to pound. I pull on my jacket with a sense of dread. What's wrong? Could he know? Oh, I so wanted this evening to be special!

"What is it?" I ask as soon as we're in the car. "Tom, what *is* it?" I am almost crying with fear. Tom, holding the wheel with both hands, stares straight ahead.

"Is it Stanford? Didn't you get in? If that's it, you might still get into Caltech, or—"

"I *got* into Stanford! That's not it at all!"

I put a hand tentatively on his arm, wishing he'd turn around and look at me in the dim light. "That's wonderful! Oh, Tom, that's wonderful!" Inside, I'm reacting to the venom in his voice, to his words. If it's not college, then he must know about me. I feel cold.

He plucks my hand off his arm as if he can't stand me, and says, "All these weeks and I never really knew a thing about you. . . ."

My eyes lock on his. "What—what do you mean?"

"How could you, Val?" His voice cracks. "You really hurt me."

Tears glide down my cheeks, and I turn away.

"That's right, cry! You're such a good actress. Tell me, can you always call up the right emotion when you want it? Is there anything honest about you?" His hurt has turned so quickly to outrage that I really cry now

79

and reach blindly for the handle of the car door. Tom grabs my arm.

"Oh no you don't! You owe me some answers, Valerie. Start talking!"

"Leave me alone!"

"Don't playact. You got your jobs through the Metzger Agency, huh? You worked for a phone answering service, huh?"

"How—how did you find out?"

"Oh, that wasn't hard at all. It's just amazing I didn't put two and two together before. I thought Betsy said something about you acting in TV commercials, but I figured that was a long time ago . . . and after all, your father's an actor!" Tom sits jammed against the door on the driver's side, eyes piercing me. "When I couldn't reach you at home yesterday, I looked up the Metzger Agency. You'd been hinting all week that you might be getting a job soon. 'Metzger *Talent* Agency . . .' the operator says. Even that didn't get through to me!"

"All right, so you know now that I'm an actress. Does that make me a freak or something? What's so terrible, my keeping it from you? If you knew, you'd have gotten all awestruck as if I were some precious museum piece. *Look, but don't touch.* You'd have gotten tongue-tied, just like every other boy who has found out."

Tom doesn't seem to hear me. "'You know how I can reach Valerie Hall?' I ask, and the operator says, 'Just a moment, I'll put you through to her agent, Josh Metzger.'"

"Josh?" My voice comes out in a squeak.

"What gets to me is that you had so little faith in me! That you manipulated me, just like your mother manipulates you! You had no regard for my feelings. You played with me like a fish on a line!" His voice breaks, and he turns his face away.

"I didn't! I never manipulated you! You're the first boy I ever cared for!"

"Oh, sure. You cared so much, you never planned to say anything about that 'other' life. How did you intend explaining where you'll be for the next two weeks? Feed me another half-truth?" He wipes a hand angrily across his eyes.

I have no answers. He's right. "You don't understand," I try, through my tears. "I was going to tell you."

"Oh, sure. When? And you're right. I don't understand! Boy, the stories I swallowed—going to dinner *for your mother*, going sailing *with friends*. . . . Did you mean anything you said?"

"Stop it! Stop it! You're distorting everything!"

"I am, am I?"

"Forget it, then! If that's what you want to believe, go ahead. You won't believe me no matter what I say now."

Crying, hurt and angry, I yank open the car door and jump out. Tom does nothing to stop me. Still hoping he'll come after me, I run the short distance to the front door and turn around. The car starts up and leaps forward, snarling down the road. Eyes blurring, I fumble in my purse for the house key, but the door opens. There's Mom, face solemn and concerned. She holds her arms out to me.

"Darling, sweet, dear child, please don't let it hurt you so," Mother croons when she hears what happened. "He's nothing but a boor to talk to you that way. What does he know about ambition and the demands of a career? If he'd had the slightest compassion instead of flying off the handle like that . . ."

I am sobbing into Mom's shoulder. She pats my back and leads me to the couch. "You'll forget all about him, just wait and see. A week . . . maybe two. You'll meet so many interesting people, be doing so many interesting things, you won't even have time to think about him."

Her words don't comfort but set me to crying even more. Suddenly I feel awful. Hot and cold and achy all over. Mom takes my temperature, and it's high. I get into bed and curl up into a small ball, pulling the comforter up around my ears, but I am so cold, my teeth chatter. Mother gives me aspirin and liquids, but all I want to do is sleep—turn off my head, numb my heart, and sleep.

Chapter 10

It is Sunday afternoon and my fever is down, but I feel empty and drained, as if everything around me is in black and white. Mother bounces around the house pretending to be in good spirits. She tries to keep me busy by reading aloud parts of the Sunday paper, or putting records on, or just chattering. I follow her with my eyes, but the rest of me is off elsewhere. I go over every word of yesterday's argument, again and again, but no matter how many times I do, I can't think of what I could have said different that would change things.

The phone rings. I leap up. "Let me," I say, hoping it's Tom. Trembling, I let the phone ring once more, then hesitantly lift the receiver. "Hello?"

There's a silence, then a deep man's voice says, "Barbara?"

"What number do you want?" My throat tightens with disappointment.

He takes a breath and says, "Sorry, must have the wrong number."

Mom, in stopped motion, hides a smile of relief and goes to get her purse and car keys. She's off to the market now that I'm feeling better.

Ten minutes later I'm boiling water for tea, still in my blue bathrobe, when the doorbell rings. Again my heart jumps.

I run to the door and, against all mother's warnings about checking the peephole, fling open the door.

It's a man in his late thirties. He is neatly dressed in a beige suit and brown shirt. He has dark brown hair tinged with gray, a rugged face with fair skin and wide-set blue eyes.

I clutch my robe to my throat. "Yes?"

He doesn't say anything at first, just stares at me. Then, finally, in a very soft, scared voice, he asks, "Valerie?"

I get hot and cold, both at once, and look over his shoulder for Mom. I know who he is but, even so, have to ask.

"Don't you know? I'd know you anywhere, even if I passed you on a crowded street in Manhattan."

"Daddy?"

He smiles now and holds his arms out to me. Without thinking, I move right into them and start laughing and blubbering all sorts of questions and statements that don't make a whole lot of sense. When he releases me, he says, "Aren't you going to ask your father in?"

"Yes, yes, of course." I lead the way, my hand in his, and talk to him over my shoulder. "Mom's gone to the market. She'll be back soon."

"I know. I watched her leave. I phoned first. Remember . . . 'Barbara'? I phoned a couple of times the last

84

few days, but every time I got Irene. Once, I said I was taking a survey. The second time, I wanted to sell her a vacuum cleaner."

"Didn't she guess?"

He laughs. It's a deep, full-throated laugh, full of delight. "First time, I was a middle-aged woman, and the second, a regular Mr. Milquetoast."

I laugh too. Mom isn't easily fooled. I guess Dad figured that if she heard his voice, she'd know immediately.

The teakettle is whistling, and he says, "See, even the kettle is glad to see me!"

I'm shy suddenly, and a little afraid. What if Mom comes home before she's due?

Dad gazes around the living room, slowly taking everything in. It's a pleasant room with a fireplace on one wall and rose-colored sofas facing each other on an off-white carpet. On the fireplace mantel are photos of me, and Mom and me.

Dad smiles. "I see Irene burned every photo she ever had of me."

"She's very bitter," I say. "You know . . . after all . . . you did run off and leave us."

He nods. "So that's how she tells it. I bet. I bet she says I never sent a penny either."

Our eyes meet, and he knows from my face that he has guessed right. I bring in a tray from the kitchen with the teapot, two cups, and some English tea biscuits. I set the tray down on the table between us and sit down to pour the tea. When I look up, Dad is watching.

"You're lovely. I'm awed. My coloring, my nose, your mother's eyes and mouth . . . and so much more talent than I ever had at your age."

"How would you know?" The heat rises to my cheeks.

"You think I wasn't interested? I read about the series you'll be in in *Daily Variety*. I scan the paper regularly for any mention of you. Why, I've followed your career from the very beginning."

"Me too!" I cry. "I clip every announcement, every review I find that mentions you!"

We sit there, across from each other, grinning. Dad reaches a hand out to me, and I take it. Then, without letting go, I change seats to sit beside him.

In the next half hour we talk nonstop. Dad tells how he left Hollywood because he wanted to act in legitimate theater, rather than in films. "I tried, honey. I really did. Between bit parts I worked as a waiter, a parking lot attendant, anything, but it wasn't going anywhere. Your mother didn't see things that way. And she didn't want to leave California. She gave me an ultimatum. Stay in Hollywood, or you'll never see Valerie again.

"I don't think she really meant to say that, but once it was out, she was too proud to back down. I gambled. I said I was leaving. She made good on her threat."

"Was it true you never sent money?"

Daddy squints in a grimace. The gesture is familiar, and then I realize it's something I do when I'm not happy with myself, yet I couldn't have learned it from him. "In the beginning there was no money to send," he says. "Later, maybe five years later, when I tried to send money, she refused to take it. I kept writing, but she never answered. I don't even know if she read the letters."

I squeeze Daddy's hand in sympathy. "Why now, Daddy? Why, after all these years, do you look for me now?"

He gazes off across the room and wrinkles his brow. "Because, knowing Irene, she's probably orchestrating your life as she tried to do mine, and you may need a referee."

"What—what do you mean?"

He turns very serious eyes to me. "A little bird told me you may not want to continue acting, that you may want to do something else with your life. You should have that right."

"Who?" Suddenly a thought comes to me. "*Maurie?*"

"It doesn't matter. The important thing is—is it true?"

"Yes, Daddy, it is. I love acting. Yes. But it's all I've ever known. I don't really know if I want to be tied down for three years with this series. I've never done anything else. Maybe I could be an artist? Or maybe I have a talent for writing, or maybe I would rather be an engineer, or a teacher, or . . . I don't know. I've never had the chance to find out." It feels so good to talk like this, knowing Dad has no ax to grind. It's so good to get an unbiased opinion.

"Have you applied to college?"

Before I can answer I hear the car enter the garage. I jump, as if someone has caught me doing something wrong, then stare in horror at Daddy. "She's home! You've got to leave! Hurry! She'll be in in a minute."

Dad rises, starts to the door, then stops. "No. I have as much right to talk to you as she has. No. I'll stay!"

"Daddy, please!"

"Relax, honey. What can your mother do to me that she hasn't already?"

I hear a door open. Mother enters the kitchen from the garage. "Valerie?" she calls. Torn between fear for my father and fear of my mother, I rush into the kitchen. "Help me unpack the groceries, will you, darling?" Mom is already on her way back to the garage for more bags. Automatically I begin to take the cans and packages out of their sacks. My mind is swirling. It's as if a time bomb is ticking away in the other room.

"I tell you, prices are going up every week. You know what I spent? Forty-seven dollars just on what you see, and none of it on meats. . . ." Mother unloads two more bags onto the kitchen counter.

"Hello, Irene."

My heart stops. Mother's eyes open wide, and her face goes white as she turns to the voice of my father. She looks from him to me, and then back to him. "Ronnie! What are you doing here?"

"I've come to see my daughter."

"What! Valerie! How could you let him in?" She puts a hand to her mouth. "Oh, my. This isn't the first time!"

"No, no, Mom. I never saw Dad before. Honestly!"

She seems to believe me; the horror in her voice has changed to fury. "How dare you come into my home! You have no right! No right to see Val! Get out! Don't dare come here again. And don't you ever try to see my daughter again, do you hear? I swear, you do, and I'll call the police!"

"Mom, please! I want to see Dad. Please. I love you both!"

"What has he been telling you, huh? What lies has he

been feeding you? He always could make up good stories. And why is he here now? Have you asked him? Looking for a piece of the pie? Is that what you're after, Ronnie?"

"Now, Irene, calm down. It's been a long time. I'm doing quite all right for myself. I don't need anything from you."

Mom looks again from me to Dad and back, and then, as if a light has gone on in her head, she smacks her hands together and cries, "Oh, that's it! Yes! I should have known. Spite, that's what it is! You know you have no claims to Valerie's income, so you're out to spite me! You're trying to charm her into going east to be near you, to ruin everything we've got going here."

"She wants to go to college, Irene. She's—"

"Get out of here! What would you know about what Val wants? Where were you when she needed you? Don't you dare interfere now. Get out of here. Now!" Mother, with the strength and fury of a lion, lunges forward on her high heels. I jump between her and Daddy and scream at her to stop. She is so angry that it's hard to hold her back. "Get out of here!" she shouts. "Out! Out!"

While I'm panting from the effort to restrain Mom, Daddy retreats. His face is ashen, and his eyes never leave Mom. Finally he is gone. I hear the front door close. Then Mom collapses into my arms and bursts into uncontrollable tears.

Chapter 11

I stay close to Mom all afternoon and evening. She needs to know every detail of Dad's visit.

"Promise me," she insists, "that you won't see him again, no matter what! Promise me!"

I promise, but a gnawing ache starts in my stomach.

"Promise," she goes on, "that you'll have nothing to do with him. He's a charmer, he is. You don't know him the way I do. He'll try to talk you into giving up everything and going away with him—just for spite!"

"Mom, Mom," I say, "I told you a dozen times already. I won't see Daddy again. I won't talk to him, no matter what. I won't go running away with him."

"Good." She sounds satisfied at last. "And one last thing. Don't even refer to him as Daddy. For a man to be a father, to deserve the name Daddy, he has to stick around. A father is someone who nurtures and loves and is there in the bad times as well as the good, not someone who runs off just because things get a little rough!"

At last she is satisfied and we can get on to other things. We've both spent a great deal of emotional energy, and, too, it's the night before I start work, so we decide to go out to dinner. We drive the short distance to the small Thai restaurant that we both like. Mom tells me stories she has picked up around the trade about each of the cast members in the series. She speaks with great animation despite the weariness I see in her eyes. So long as she gets her way, life can return to normal.

It's not until late the same evening, when I'm alone at last, that I can think. And then it hits me—the sense that nothing's right, that I really have no control over my own life. When I try to pin down why I feel this way, it comes down to Tom, Daddy, Mom, the series. It's over with Tom, I think; even if we do see each other again, it will never be the same. I want to see Daddy again, but I've made a promise to Mom and she deserves my loyalty. The series. I should be looking forward to doing it; it's a real stretch professionally. But three years! And what about college?

I get nowhere in my thinking.

Make lists. That always helps push aside what hurts or worries me. So I write: "Wash hair, pack school-books to take along, set out jeans, pink sweater for tomorrow, set alarm for seven. Reread script, how to play scene with Jamey?"

The night seems endless. At one o'clock I go into the kitchen for a half glass of milk. Finally I sleep.

Josh is at the door promptly at eight. He wants to be sure everything will go smoothly. From tomorrow on I will drive or take a cab.

"Come in, Josh," Mother says. "Have a cup of coffee. There's time."

"No, thanks, Mrs. Hall. I think we should be on our way. Get there a little early the first day." Josh leans against the door frame watching me with a kind of bemused concern. "Feeling okay, Val?" he asks.

Day pack over one shoulder, I nod. *Do I look as tired as I feel?*

"I don't see why I can't come! I should be on the set with Val!"

"I assumed you'd be working, Mrs. Hall. And anyway, it's better not to this first week. Either I'll fill in as her guardian, or one of the production assistants. The director's not fond of mothers—"

"*I never!*"

"Of course, you'd never interfere with the director's instructions. I didn't say that, but you know how some of those ambitious stage moms can be. . . ." Josh smiles at Mother and reaches a hand out for my pack.

"Let's go, Val."

We stride down the path to his car, not talking. I'm sure Mom is watching. Knowing her, she might decide to come along regardless of what Josh says. I climb into the car and look back. She blows me a kiss, then starts toward the car, calling some last-minute instructions, I suppose, but Josh speeds away.

"What's wrong?" he asks on the way to the studio. He glances at me appraisingly as we stop at a traffic light. "Your mother?"

I shake my head.

"Trouble with a boyfriend, maybe? This guy Tom Gordon who phoned Friday?"

I nod.

"I'm sorry. Is he important?"

His concern makes me choke up, and I nod again.

"First love?"

I don't answer.

"I'm sorry, really. I got the impression that I made him angry, but I can't think why. All I said was that I was your agent and would be happy to relay his message to you; then I asked his name."

"He told me and said he was your friend, then he asked what I meant by *agent*. I told him you were an actress and that you'd be starting work on a pilot next week, without thinking how strange it was that he was a friend and didn't seem to know about your work. 'Didn't you know?' I asked. 'No . . . apparently not,' he said. I realized then I'd said too much. Hope it hasn't created trouble between you." He glances at me. "Oh-oh, guess it has."

I begin to cry quietly, and Josh reaches under the dash to pull out a wad of tissues which he hands to me, without looking. I turn away from him, embarrassed, and continue to cry. A Beethoven symphony is playing on the tape deck, and Josh listens in silence, giving me time to pull myself together. When I'm finally in control, he says, "You know, Val, I've told you, I'd like to be your friend. So if there's anything you want to talk about, to get an unbiased opinion . . . I'm a good listener."

As we drive onto the San Diego freeway, heading over the pass into west L.A., I tell him about the mess of lies and half-truths I told Tom. And about boys I knew before him. "Every time I'd get interested in a boy and he found out I was an actress, he'd change," I say. "Once, the boy I went with just got so tongue-tied and self-conscious, as if I was a goddess or something . . . and another time the boy went around boasting to everyone that he was dating an *actress*."

Josh nods in understanding.

"I just wanted to have a normal relationship, like other girls my age. And it was going so well with Tom. For the first time in my whole life I felt that someone cared about me just because of *me*."

Eyes on the road, Josh says, "He'll get over it. Give him time. I'm sure he values you for your sensitivity, your sense of humor, your thoughtfulness—for all your very nice qualities. From what you say, he's an intelligent fellow. When he gets over the hurt that you didn't give him the whole truth . . . he'll be back."

"Do you really think so?"

He smiles my way and touches my hand reassuringly. "Absolutely."

The tightness in my chest eases. Maybe tonight Tom will phone, and I'll tell him all about my first day at work, about all the others actors and actresses. Maybe the awkwardness will wear off if I talk about my work the way it really is—hard, repetitious, and very tiring.

"Now," Josh says, pulling down the sun visor on my side so I can use the mirror, "see what you can do with those teary eyes, and spruce up that pretty face. Bill

94

Korbel likes his actresses bright-eyed and bushy-tailed."
He pauses. "A terrible cliché; *his* words, not mine."

"Is he married to a squirrel?"

He starts to laugh. And then, suddenly, I'm laughing too.

The series is about teenagers at Beverly High—about their loves, family and peer relationships, and problems. The producers are sure it's going to appeal to a large teen audience, that it will grab them away from other prime-time TV. And I suppose it might. Each episode deals with some important question.

We—the cast for this pilot episode which will be used to sell the idea to the networks—sit around a long conference table getting acquainted. The producer, director, and story editor are there too. "Valerie Hall plays Andrea," Bill Korbel, the director, says. "She's ingenuous, sweet, eager for life, and she's never been in love before. In this first episode . . ."

One by one the director tells us how he sees each of our parts. He encourages us to get to know one another so we'll be a "family." "After all," he says, "you'll be working together for a long time . . . we hope."

Josh sits off to the side, watching and listening. I forget he's there, because I become so absorbed in those around me. Brian, the boy I'm going to fall hard for, gives the impression of being a real jock. You know, broad shoulders, six one, a neck like a telephone pole, an easy smile. Marissa, my best friend in the series, seems to be eyeing him with more than casual interest. Jamey, the "nice" boy, wears glasses and is tall and skinny; he's the kind you would expect to find in the chemistry lab or running track—intense, genuine. The mother and father roles are played by known actors. All in all, they're an interesting bunch. And I wonder if any of them are really like the characters they portray.

By noon we've finished our second read-through. The story editor wants to make some changes because some of the lines read awkwardly. We'll get the changes right after the lunch break.

Josh joins me as soon as the director calls lunch. "Looks good. I don't think you'll need me, so I'm going to head back to the office. Hal will look after you. Pick you up about five. Okay?"

"Sure, Josh, and thanks. I really appreciate everything."

"That's okay, kid," he says, imitating Humphrey Bogart, and then he salutes and leaves.

Marissa, Brian, Jamey, and I start down the hall to the commissary. We chatter about our parts, about the roles we played before, about the director . . . and I get the sense that it will be fun working with these kids. I'm just about to follow Marissa into the commissary, thinking how glad I am that I won't have to eat yucky fried chicken or lasagna, the stuff you usually have for lunch when caterers serve film crews on location, when I think I hear my name.

Jamey touches my arm. "Say, Valerie. That guy over there is calling you."

I turn around. Hurrying toward me, an anxious look on his face . . . is my father.

Chapter 12

"Daddy!" I separate myself from the others and run to
him. "What are you doing here?" I look around in confusion, half expecting to see Mom rushing down the hall
or studio police coming after him.

"You want us to wait?" Jamey calls out.

"No . . . go on in. I'll be with you in a minute."

Daddy and I face each other, and I'm thinking a hundred things at once. That I'm not supposed to be talking
to him; that it's amazing he got into the studio with
security so tight; and that I'm so glad to see him.

The producer and director go by, deep in conversation, nodding vague acknowledgment at me. As someone opens the commissary door the aroma of coffee
leaks out, and the sounds of many voices.

"I want to talk to you," Daddy says. "I won't take
much of your time. Is there someplace quiet nearby?"

"Uh . . . er . . . maybe the conference room. Everybody
should be gone by now." I walk briskly back in the

direction of the room where our meeting took place, Dad at my side. The story editor is just leaving, a pack of scripts in hand. A man is removing ashtrays and refilling water pitchers.

"Could we use this room for a few minutes?" I ask.

The man looks from me to Dad, sweeps the last ashtray into a basket, and leaves. Daddy closes the door and pulls out a chair for me before sitting down perpendicular to me.

"I know you're not supposed to talk to me anymore, Val. I'm sorry to compromise you like this. But I had to see you once more. I'm leaving for Boston tonight," he says.

"Oh!" The word comes out in a squeak of disappointment.

"I realize what a shock it must have been to Irene seeing me after all these years, thinking I was trying to win you away from her. But believe me, that's not why I came. She's right. I wasn't much of a father. Maybe I could have tried harder to keep in touch . . . sent money sooner . . . I don't know."

I am drinking in his every word, every gesture. The muscle under his left eye twitches. Mine does that, too, whenever I'm very upset. How many other gestures, habits, ways of seeing things, does he have that I have too?

"The past is gone. I can't change what was. I can only control the present. What I want to say is that, regardless of Irene, I want to keep in touch. It's not up to her, anyway. It's your choice, or should be. I don't want to take anything from your mother. I just want to give, somehow to make up."

"I don't need anything, Daddy."

"No?" Daddy's eyes probe mine, and I sense he reads me better than Mom. "That's not the impression I got yesterday. I think you need an ally, an unbiased ear . . ."

I feel all choked up, but it's too late to back out. I signed a contract. "It doesn't make much sense giving up all this"—I gesture around the room—"all the opportunity and money, the chance to make it big . . . for college. I'd be forgotten in four years. I'd have outgrown teen roles and have to start all over again making a name for myself."

"Sounds like you're quoting Irene directly. Right?"

"Well, isn't it true?"

"Truth is many-faceted, Val, like a diamond, and it's just as likely to have flaws. What's the truth of why I left fifteen years ago? Is it what your mother says, or what I say? Is it somewhere in between, or is it many reasons that neither your mother nor I will admit?" He puts a hand on mine. "Why must there be only one way, or the other? Couldn't there be a middle ground?"

"Like what?"

"Keep your career going *and* go to school."

"I've thought of that. It would only work if I went to UCLA, and Mom would want me to live at home. Even if I didn't, and went to live in a dorm, it would still be L.A. and I'd be too close to home."

"Don't rule it out, Val. Think about it. Years ago, just to prove I could think for myself, I chose the most drastic escape. I could have taken jobs in little theater in L.A. just as well . . ."

"Little theater in L.A. isn't like New York."

Dad shrugs. "If you really love acting, stay with it.

But if you have any doubts, take a few years off and find out what it is you do love."

His encouragement gives me a surge of hope. "We couldn't afford it, though . . . going east."

"I can help."

"Mom won't let you."

"*You*'ll let me. And Irene could get a better-paying job. She's taken the least challenging work she could find to make herself available to you. It's a shame. She's a crack at organizing. She knows the ins and outs of the industry better than anyone I know. It's time she put some of that know-how and energy into her own career."

"Do you really think so?" There is both hope and doubt in my voice. Dad nods.

"And as for being forgotten in four years, it's possible, certainly. But think of what you'd gain. Exposure to new ideas and experiences would bring you greater insight and depth. Maybe you'd be a *better* actress after college, better than you are now or could ever be."

He seems so sincere, so genuinely concerned, but Mom's warning voice rings in my head: *"He's just conning you. Don't you see that? All he wants is to steal you away from me! If he was so concerned, where was he before, before you made it?"*

"You should be getting back to your friends, honey," Dad says, putting a hand on mine. "It's important to establish good rapport with them from the very beginning. . . ."

Tears spring to my eyes, and I think how important it could have been if he himself had established that kind of rapport with me, from the beginning.

"No matter what you decide, Val, I want you to know one thing. I love you very much." His voice catches. Mom would say, *"He's an actor, after all."* "If you should need me—for anything—here's my address. Phone me. Write me. I'll get back to you no matter where I may be working."

I take his card and look at the simple printing, without really seeing it.

"If you'll let me, I want to be part of your life. Will you stay in touch?"

I see his face dimly through the tears brimming in my eyes, but I try to memorize every feature, every detail. He gets up, and I do too.

"Yes, Daddy. I'll stay in touch," I say. And then he hugs me very hard, and I feel wetness on my cheek that isn't mine. Hand in hand we leave the room and walk back down the hall to the commissary.

"Good-bye, honey."

"Good-bye, Daddy . . ."

I watch him stride down the hall. He does not look back, this tall, dignified man—*my* father. And then I open the door to the commissary and go in.

On the way home I tell Josh all about the actors and actresses in the series and how we got along. And then I say, "My father was there . . . and we talked."

"Oh?" Josh gives me a surprised look which says, *How come? I thought you weren't supposed to talk to him?* and a couple of other things I can't decipher.

"How do you suppose he got in?" I ask. "Who could have gotten him a pass?"

Josh shrugs and thinks a while before saying, "Maybe

my father. He always liked your dad. He used to say that your parents were just two strong-willed kids who thought they could outbluff each other, and lost. Love has a flip side, you know." He glances at me quickly, then back to the road. "Remember that when you have to play a wife who has been badly hurt by her husband, someday . . ."

Josh will make a better agent than Maurie, I think. He would have made a good college professor, too, I think. "Josh? What do you think I should do? Should I give all this up and go on to college?"

"You're under contract now."

"I know, but after the pilot is made?"

He's quiet for a long moment, then says, "Almost anyone can go to college. Very few people have the talent to get to where you are."

"*You* went to college! You sound as if you don't believe in it!"

He seems to be choosing his words very carefully when he answers, finally. "I went to college because I wasn't talented in anything special, because I didn't know what else to do with my life."

"You mean, you think I should stick with what I'm doing."

"I think you should stop agonizing over your decision. You made your choice. You signed the contract. It's a good decision."

"But was it *my* decision?"

"Does it matter?"

"Yes."

"For heaven's sake, don't bite your nose off to spite your face. Your mother may be right, you know. Does it

102

occur to you that maybe your father's reasons aren't so pure either? He hasn't seen you for years, and unless you go east to school he won't see you for a lot more years."

"It's so complicated! Everyone's got a reason for wanting me to do what they want. Even you!"

Josh doesn't answer.

"What about it, Josh? Are you trying to talk me into staying here because it's better for me—or better for the agency?" As soon as the words are out I regret them.

Josh grips the wheel so hard, his hands turn white. I press my back against the car door and watch him anxiously. Finally he says, "Valerie. What you do should be what *you* want to do, not what anyone else urges you to do. What *do* you want?"

"I don't know for sure!"

"Well, you better find out fast because I consider a contract between our agency and a production company a binding agreement. And I thought you were professional enough to think the same!"

Chapter 13

Josh's words leave a deep impression. I *am* a professional. It's time to stop seesawing. The contract is signed. I'm already working. It's time to stop agonizing.

It's not as if I'm being forced into this *marriage*. I've loved acting for a long time. College is like a fantasy lover whom I imagine to be perfect. Why tease myself with what might be when I already have so much?

And so, on Tuesday, not having heard from Tom or phoned him, I go off to work with a more positive attitude. I feel *bright-eyed* and *bushy-tailed*, just the way the director likes it.

When I come into the rehearsal hall, which is where we meet this second day, Larry Stokes, who plays Brian, sidles up to me. He is holding out a cup of coffee like a bouquet of flowers, and his deep-set eyes are teasing.

"Why, thanks," I say, pleased at the thoughtfulness.

He maneuvers me against a wall, and I peer around him for the director. "Korbel's not here yet," Larry—or *Brian*, as I think of him—says. "Thought we should get to know each other a little better. After all, we have that dynamite scene together."

He means the scene in which we bump into each other for the first time and I have to get across to the audience the strong attraction I instantly feel.

"Doesn't look like you'll have any problem playing *your* part," I say. "You have the appeal of three guys put together."

"You noticed." He lights a cigarette, and his eyes glide over to me. He's extremely attractive and he knows it. I feel both embarrassed and angry and search for a way to turn him off.

"Tell me about yourself," I say, figuring the one thing that will divert him is talking about what is probably his favorite subject.

An actor since he was a toddler, at the age of six he was already taking two hours of dance class a day, two of ice-skating, as well as horseback riding, acting, and karate classes.

"But it was worth it," he says. "I got lots of parts. And I know *everyone*. Want to meet . . ." And he rattles off the names of some of the best-known actors and directors. "Only now . . ." He leaves the sentence dangling and shrugs as if it's not really important. But I suddenly understand.

There are some actors who, when they're young, are pushed so hard to be "cute" that they never learn to be anything else. And one day, suddenly, they're too big for cute-kid parts. They're adolescents. Then what?

By the time we rejoin the others, I have very mixed feelings about Brian. Dislike for his boasting. Admiration for his dogged determination. And . . . fear. Our backgrounds are so similar that I wonder if others see me the way I see him.

Except those aren't the emotions I'm supposed to feel or show in my first scene with him.

"Let's take that from the top one more time, Andrea. It's not quite right," Korbel calls out. "I want to see you blush. I want to see confusion."

We're rehearsing the scene in which I first meet Brian; I'm pushing along down a crowded school hall when I hear Marissa calling. The script calls for me to turn around and run smack-dab into him.

I take my position, books clutched in hand. Korbel calls "Action" even though the cameraman won't be involved until Thursday, when they practice the angles they'll shoot Friday in front of a live audience. I close my eyes for an instant to hype myself into the proper emotional mood. It's the third time we've rehearsed this scene, and I can't seem to get it right.

"Andrea!" (It's Marrissa's voice.)

I stop, turn my head in the direction of the voice, then turn. I bump right into Brian. He puts his arms around me. I look up at him. He's amused, knowing.

"Hey!" I say. Brian looks me over, gives me a cool approving smile. I drop a book. He picks it up.

"You're going the wrong way, *Andrea*," Brian says, getting my name from the book cover. He puts his hands on my shoulders and turns me around like a stick doll.

This is the place where the camera will close in on my

reaction. I should be stunned, awestruck, and horrified at my own reaction.

"Cut!"

I jump away and look anxiously at Korbel.

"What's wrong, Valerie?" he asks. "You know what I want. What's the matter? Haven't you ever had an instant attraction to someone? Plug into the feeling. That's what I want to see. Now, come on. Let's do it again."

I'm annoyed with myself. Where's my professionalism? So what if I think of Brian as an empty, pathetic, overgrown kid who thinks he's God's gift to women. In this scene I'm meeting him for the first time, so how would I even know that?

"I'm sorry. I just wasn't concentrating," I say. Mom, who has taken an extra hour off for lunch and is standing behind Korbel, looks upset, and this triggers my adrenaline.

Brian and I assume the same positions as before. I readjust my books. Again I close my eyes, but this time I think about Tom and how it was that first time we met, how it feels every time we meet. I know now one of the emotions I have to show.

"Action!" Korbel calls out again.

This time I do it right. I can feel it. I'm *in* Andrea's skin now. When we finish the scene, I turn to Korbel, knowing I was good. He smiles and holds his raised thumb and forefinger in a circle. "That's my girl," he says. "Let's go on to the next scene now."

Two acceptance letters come in the same week, from UCLA and Cornell. When I tell Mom, she says, "Don't torture yourself, honey. You made your decision. Just toss them away."

"I can't!"

She shrugs and turns aside.

I hurriedly rip open the UCLA letter, saving the important one for last. UCLA accepts. A smile of pleasure grows inside me. Then fearfully I open the letter from Cornell.

I've wanted to go to that college in upper New York State ever since I found out that Dad lived in New York, and saw pictures of the campus which showed Gothic buildings on hilly slopes against a backdrop of blue skies, with trees and bushes in full fall colors.

I've lived in Southern California all my life, so I've never experienced seasons. Winter, spring, summer, and fall here are pretty much all alike. In January it can be warm enough to go swimming; flowers and trees bloom then, too.

My heart leaps at the thought of tramping through thick layers of red and gold leaves; of going to football games bundled up in warm clothes; of tasting the first snow and making snowballs; of seeing those first pale buds of spring and smelling wet, rich earth.

Mom clears her throat. "Well?"

"They both accepted me."

"Congratulations." There is a tremor in her voice.

I take the letters into my bedroom to savor all the details. Even though I won't be going to college, I do want to share my news. Of course, it's Tom I think of first, but I'm scared. He hasn't phoned me yet; what if he hangs up on me?

Instead I call Suzie. Before I can even tell her my

news she's bubbling over with her own. She just got a part in a daytime soap. She's in love. "Didn't you get my message?" she asks. I glance at my answering machine and note that the light's on.

"Of course you got in," she says enthusiastically when I tell her. "I never doubted that, did you?"

"I have four weeks to decide."

"Well, goodness, Val," she says. "Why wait? You know what you're going to do!"

"Of course. Sure." I bring the subject back to work, and Suzie promises to attend the videotaping tomorrow.

As soon as I hang up I rewind the message tape and listen. The first message is Suzie's, telling me the news I just heard. The second is Mrs. Moffat asking me to call her. The third is Tom. I get all fluttery and scared when I hear him say, *"Val, this is Tom. Could you please phone? I need to talk to you."*

He called! Oh, my gosh, he called! That's all I can think, and I pick up the receiver, quivering with fear, to dial him.

It takes two of his hellos before I find the breath to answer.

"Val?"

"Yes . . ."

"Oh, great! I'm so glad. I was afraid you might not call. How are you?"

"Fine. How are you?"

Pause. "Better, now that I'm talking to you. I wanted to phone a dozen times but figured you'd never want to talk to me after the way I jumped all over you."

"I should have told you the truth from the first."

"I should have given you a chance to explain."

"It's so good to hear your voice!"

"And yours . . ."

For a moment neither of us says anything. My mouth is dry, and I'm grinning foolishly at the bedspread, and I wish Tom were right next to me at this moment. And then we both start talking at once, not even listening to what the other says, just spilling out all the things we've been saving up to share.

"Hold it!" Tom cries out at last.

I stop babbling.

"This is crazy. I've got to see you. There's so much to say. I want to hear what you've been doing. I've just got to see you!"

"*Me too!*"

"I'll be right over!"

"Mom will kill me! Tomorrow's the taping and I'm supposed to get to bed early."

There's what I guess is called a pregnant pause, and then I say, "Oh, what the heck. If she kills me, I won't be able to work tomorrow, and that would kill her." We both giggle. "Hurry up! I'm not very good at waiting!"

When the bell rings, Mom starts to the door, but I intercept her. "It's Tom," I say. "We're going out for a while."

"What? *Valerie!* Tomorrow's the taping!"

I give Mom a quick peck on the cheek and brush by her. "See you later. Don't worry. And don't stay up waiting." I open the door to Mom's rising protests and close it without a flicker of guilt. Tom's eyes light up, and we give each other a big, joyous hug. Then, hand in hand, we run down the path to his car.

110

There's so much to catch up on. He tells me all about what's happening at school, and about his huge family. (He's the middle one of five children, and something's always happening.) I tell him about the role I'm playing, and about the actors and actresses I'm working with, and that I'll be back at school next week. His face lights up at that news, and he asks lots of questions.

"I'd like to come see you," he says finally.

"You really would?"

"Sure. Can I come to the taping tomorrow? What's it like?"

I almost burst with happiness. He's treating everything I tell him as if it's the most normal activity in the world, as if he's asking to watch me compete in an everyday swim meet.

I explain about the soundstage where the taping will take place, and about the padded walls that shut out outside noise. I tell him about the warm-up person who will talk to the audience before the show starts, to get them in the right mood. About the huge robotlike videotape cameras the operators ride. And about the big TV sets hung over and in front of the seats.

"The director will be in the control room watching little TV screens," I explain. "He decides which camera angles to use. *And afterward we're having a party*." I don't even hesitate when I ask, "Will you come?"

"Sure!"

"Oh, Tom!" I fling myself into his arms, so full of relief and delight I am shivering. Maybe it will be all right, after all. Maybe Tom won't be threatened by my work, as other boys were. He has a sense of his own worth the others lacked. It's going to be okay!

111

It isn't until I get home after midnight that I realize I never said a word about Cornell. I giggle at the thought. After all, that *was* the reason I phoned him, wasn't it?

"Valerie?" Mom calls. "Is that you?"

"Yes, Mom."

"It's very late!"

"I know, Mom. Good night." Still smiling, I open the door to my bedroom and flop down on my bed. I'm not sure I'll be able to sleep at all tonight.

Chapter 14

The taping of the pilot takes almost two hours although it will only run about forty-five minutes, with fifteen minutes more devoted to commercials. It goes smoothly from start to finish, and when it's over, the audience gives us a big hand, not just because the applause screen lights up, but because they really seem to like it. Tom and Suzie, sitting beside each other the way I arranged, applaud wildly, and then Marissa calls to tell me everyone's going in to the party.

Still in makeup and wardrobe, the two of us join the others in a room decorated with balloons and streamers. Tables are laid out with cheeses, sandwiches, and drinks. Everyone's congratulating everyone else or telling someone how great they were. Very quickly the place fills up with cast and production crew—cameramen, sound and lighting people, makeup and wardrobe people, writers, assistants, and assistants to the assistants.

Brian joins us. "So, what do you guys think? Will the network buy it?"

"Who knows . . ." I keep my eyes on the door expecting to see Tom and Suzie any second.

"I care. It matters a lot to me . . ."

"Me too," Marissa says, and I wander off, making my way to the door. I greet people, accept their congratulations and compliments, knowing that everyone says nice things whether they mean it or not. I'm very high with the excitement of having done my job well and the sense of comradeship with everyone around me.

I'm almost to the door when the director passes, talking to one of his assistants: ". . . don't know about him. Still hasn't grown up. Can't shed that cute-kid image. That suave veneer reads false to me. Underneath he's . . ."

He moves on. Is he talking about Brian? Don't they like him? What will happen if they drop his option? He has pinned so much hope on becoming a regular in the series!

Ahead I see Tom and Suzie looking for me. Suzie's eyes shine. She loves these kinds of parties and knows lots of the people here. Tom has that awestruck look that turns a knife in my stomach. Maybe it was a mistake inviting him here. I rush over to them and grab his hand. "Come on! I'll introduce you to everyone."

Someone calls Suzie, and she peels off to talk shop while I steer Tom to the food tables, chattering at twice my normal pace about how the taping went. Did he notice how Brian flubbed a line and I covered for him by changing my dialogue? What did he think of it all? How did he like the part I played?

With drinks in hand I pilot him to Marissa, Brian, and Jamey who are talking with a couple of production people. When there's a lull in the conversation, I say, "Hey, guys, I'd like you to meet a friend of mine—Tom Gordon." I link arms with him. "Tom, this is Pauline, Larry, and Stuart." I name each of the other people in our circle. Tom politely holds out a hand, but only Stuart—Jamey—takes it.

"So, as I was saying"—Brian turns back to the lighting men—"when I was in *Low Riders*—remember that picture? I played a nine-year-old hood? Well, they did these weird things with lights."

For a while we stand there. Everyone seems to have something to say about an experience in some film, and I try to think of a way to include Tom in the conversation. I touch Jamey's arm. "Tom's going to Stanford in the fall. He's going to study physics . . ."

"Oh, yeah?" Jamey says. "That's nice." And he turns his attention back to the conversation about lighting.

"Didn't you tell me you were going to school at night, Jamey?" I try again.

"Huh? Oh . . . yeah. That was in the fall. I work nights now as a parking lot attendant so I can be free days for calls. If we get the go-ahead for the series, I'll be able to quit my night job . . ." He smiles. End of conversation.

"They're doing some amazing things with lasers now to create different lighting effects," Tom offers.

The lighting men are interested, and for a few moments attention shifts to Tom, but he gets too technical, and soon I see a vague look in people's eyes. Brian is already scouting the crowd for someone else who might listen to him.

After that we stay pretty much on our own. Now and then someone comes over to say how much he or she enjoyed working with me, and I introduce Tom, but the conversation doesn't go anywhere. It's as if he's from a foreign country and can't speak our language. He tries, and at times some remark seems to inspire a real dialogue, but never for long. Part of me is angry that some of my so-called friends are outright rude. And part of me is worried that Tom and I are living in such different worlds that we'll never be able to make it together.

"You have to realize," I try to explain later, hoping to gloss over the awkwardness. "It's like a select club. A lot of these guys socialize with each other outside of the job too. Their lives are completely wrapped up in film."

"Sure," Tom says good-naturedly. "Talk to a bunch of physicists and it would be pretty much the same."

"Oh, Tom, you understand!" I exclaim, and I give him a joyful kiss.

Monday it's back to life as usual. The gang at school is interested in what it was like for me . . . for all of about two minutes. Then it's as if it never happened. The talk goes to teachers and friends and movies seen over the weekend, and the senior prom. And I like it that way.

Wherever did I get the idea that I'd be a freak if people knew more about what I do?

For all its normalcy, part of me has gone underground. The final date for responding to UCLA and Cornell is in three weeks. By the last of those weeks I am in a perpetual state of anxiety. I have these debates with myself all the time. *Should I? Shouldn't I? Do I want to or not?*

The acceptance forms are sitting in my desk drawer. They almost glow in the dark. Every night in this last week I take them out to read. I browse through the catalogues, pretending that I'm plotting my schedule: *This course and this course look interesting*. In my imagination I even "walk" through the campus to the different buildings. I think about weekends in New York, with Daddy. We'll go to the museums, walk along Fifth Avenue together, have lunch in Greenwich Village. Oh, I want that kind of freedom, so much!

One day I phone Josh and ask if we couldn't have coffee someplace to talk. I'm not even sure what I will say to him, relying on my subconscious to come through at the right moment.

Josh picks me up at Moffat's the same day and drives me to a wonderful pastry shop in Beverly Hills. He orders a cappuccino for himself and a café au lait for me. Plus two extraordinarily calorific pastries. He chatters on about some juicy celebrity gossip and amuses me with more Hollywood trivia. Then he takes my hand. "Okay, Val. What's up? Want to unburden yourself on your old uncle Josh?"

The picture of Josh as my old uncle is so outlandish that I laugh, but the laughter is very close to tears. Good old Josh is right there with the tissues again.

"I want to go to college, Josh. What should I do?"

He draws in his breath and groans like someone who's been punched in the stomach.

I put my hand on his. "Can I get out of the contract?"

117

"Don't do that, Val, please."

"I want to. Oh, I want to so much. All I think about is going, getting away, finding out if I'm any more than a chameleon."

"Val, please. You're an actress, and a good one. You've got a combination of wistfulness, radiance, and yearning. You've got so much going for you." He takes my hand, very absorbed suddenly in the vein that runs down the back of it. When he looks up, he says, "And it's not just because you're so talented that I want you to stay."

A curious mix of emotions race across his face. With sudden insight I realize that Josh really cares for me, and not just as my agent. I want to touch him, comfort him, but he would not want sympathy, so I pretend not to understand. He is such a good friend, such a nice person, I wish I could feel the same.

He shakes his head and smiles. "Never mind . . . that's my problem. Now tell me what changed your mind."

"Larry Stokes," I say. "Larry's never known any other life than acting, and neither have I. He's at a crossroads now too. If he can't make the transition from kid star to grown-up, he's finished. The industry doesn't care that he gave so much of his life to it. They'll just say, 'Bye-bye, good luck.' What else is he good for?"

"But you're not Larry Stokes. You have talent. You could go far."

"But as whom? As Andrea the teenage ingenue? As Joyce the anorexic? I'm a chameleon, Josh! I take on the colors of whomever I play. *Who am I?*"

"You're Valerie Hall. Talented, intelligent, sensitive—"

I cut him off with an impatient sweep of my hand. "Don't. Please. It's all a lot of words, a lot of logic. I know what I want, what I *feel*. If I don't listen to those feelings, I'll always be sorry."

"Three years from now . . ."

"Three years from now it will be too late. I'll have *become* whatever it is the industry expects me to be. I'll be twenty, twenty-one, too old to be a freshman. Don't you see?"

He nods, but his eyes are cloudy.

"What can I *do?*"

"Let me think a minute." He closes his eyes for an instant, then opens them. "Go ahead and accept whatever school you want. You'd only lose your deposit if you change your mind."

"I won't change it."

"The network may not like the pilot. Then again, they *may* like the pilot and not want you for the main part. But I think they will. Like both you *and* the pilot. Just brainstorming, so don't stop me."

I nod.

"You'll be in hot water if you back out now. Wait."

"How long?"

"Until we hear from the network. If they want to go ahead, *do* the first six episodes. *Then* we'll talk about breaking the contract."

"You're not trying to con me, are you? I mean, six episodes will take me into the third week of school!"

"I'm not trying to con you, Val."

"*Then* what?"

"With six episodes, plus a pilot on tape, you'll have a track record; your reputation will be established."

"And then?"

"Then, if the network gives the go-ahead for the *next* seven episodes, we get the writers to write you out . . . an accident, a fatal illness, or maybe even going off to college. Leave it to them."

"I'll be blacklisted," I say sadly. "Even if I want to, I'll never be able to work in the industry again, will I?"

He closes both of his hands over mine and smiles. "Honey, there's one thing about the film industry that you should know."

"What?"

"Actually, two. First, you're only as good as your last picture. Second, they'll never hire you again if you cross them—*unless they need you.*"

I laugh. "Are you sure?"

"Absolutely." His face suddenly lights up. "We could get you short-term contracts. Commercials. Appearances. That sort of thing. On the East Coast, and back here." He smiles. "We could fly you in. Maybe even do a few episodes during Thanksgiving or Christmas break! Hey. I wonder if they'd go for that!"

Immediately my hopes soar. If Josh gets me jobs out here, maybe I can see Tom more often!

"If we keep you in the public eye, when you graduate—in three years, maybe—you can pick up where you left off. That is, if you still want to."

"Oh, Josh! I adore you! You're the most brilliant agent in the whole wide world." Impulsively I reach across the table and kiss him on the forehead. His face reddens.

When I settle back in my seat, Josh says, "There's one other problem to deal with, so don't let's celebrate yet."

I look up at him quizzically.

"Now that we've conspired to jettison your career in midstream, the big question is—How will you break this happy news to your mother?"

Chapter 15

I decide to put off telling Mom that I'm planning to go to Cornell. It's not an easy decision. All my life we've been as close as sisters. I've shared every thought, worry, and experience with her. Now, suddenly, I'm keeping the most important decision of my life to myself just because I can't bear the pain it will cause her. How will she manage without me? How will she survive without seeing me every day, talking things through, planning.

And how will I survive?

A small fear sits in the pit of my stomach as I fill out the Cornell forms. *"Room assignment:* Do you smoke? Play stereo late at night? Prefer a roommate of your own religious background? *Student activities:* The activities card admits you to all athletic events and allows reduced rates for on-campus theater and films."

A whole life apart from Mom.

Despite a pang of fear I make out a check to reserve my admission, and drop the thick envelope in the mail.

The weeks to graduation, spent mostly with Tom, run together in a warm blur. He's glad about Cornell and happier still that I may be back in California more often than we planned. If Josh has anything to do with it.

"I think he's got a crush on you," Tom says one of those rare times when we have the house to ourselves. Mom is at an opening with Maurie and his gang.

"Who?"

"Santa Claus." He puts a tape on the tape deck. "Who else were we talking about?"

"If you mean Josh," I say from my comfortable perch on the couch where I am sorting tapes, "he's old enough to be my uncle."

"He doesn't look at you the way an uncle does."

"Tom!" I exclaim, reaching my arms out to him. "You poor neglected male! Come here to Mama . . ."

He grins and drops down on the couch but doesn't touch me. "Are you sure you're not even a *little* in love with him?"

"Josh?"

"No, Santa Claus."

The lightness of the moment is gone. He's really serious. I think for a moment and realize that I do like Josh. And admire him. And respect him. And feel safe and comfortable with him. But that's all. "Actually," I say, "I'm quite crazy about Santa Claus. But as for Josh . . ."

"Oh, you!" Tom pulls me close and laughs.

"Of course," I say teasingly, head nestled against his shoulder, "I don't know how I'll feel about him *in a couple of years . . .*"

Instead of the expected kiss we tickle each other and

123

laugh until I'm close to tears. And I can't imagine ever loving anyone the way I do Tom.

The network people inform the producer who phones Maurie, who tells Josh, that they're going ahead with the series. Late in the summer we're to start shooting six episodes. If those go, there'll be more. Further, they want me in the role of Andrea.

"What about Brian?" I ask when Josh phones the news.

"Valerie! Didn't you hear me? You got the part! They loved the pilot!"

"But what about Brian?"

"They're replacing him."

"What!"

Josh didn't answer.

"That's *rotten*. That's *disgusting*. All these years he's given the industry! How can they do that to him?"

"It seems the wife of one of the potential sponsors didn't like him. Said he looked like an overgrown kid hood."

"Oh, *no!*" I remember the time a producer put his arm around me after an audition and said, "Val, I love you. The part's yours. I'll talk contract with Metzger Monday." When Monday came, I learned someone else got the part. A cousin or aunt or someone thought I wasn't right. The producer didn't even have the courtesy to call me.

"What will he do?" I ask.

"He'll get other jobs," Josh says softly. "He'll be okay."

"I guess. But what a rotten business this is. You've got

to have a skin as thick as an elephant's, yet we're supposed to be supersensitive. I'm *glad* I'm going away!"

"I'm not," Josh says.

I shrug at the phone.

"Have you told your mother yet?"

"There's plenty of time—almost three months before I have to leave."

"No. There's not a lot of time. You'll be starting work soon. I have to tell Dad so he can deal with the network people. And once Dad knows, word will get back pretty fast to your mom."

"Just a little more time, Josh, please."

"Look, Val. What are you worried about? The worst that can happen is she'll blow like Mount Saint Helens. That's what I expect Dad to do."

I let out my breath in a big worried sigh. "You're right. But give me a week. I promise I'll talk to her somehow in the next week."

Mom is ecstatic over the news about the series. To celebrate, we "take" lunch at the Bistro. It's not a restaurant either of us goes to often; in fact, the only other time I ate there was with Maurie, when a producer footed the bill.

I will tell Mom right after lunch.

We order lobster salad and Perrier and while the waiter writes it all down, Mom informs him and anyone nearby who can hear that I am her daughter and we are celebrating. "She's just gotten a wonderful part in a TV series directed by Bill Korbel. You've heard of him?"

The waiter smiles, pad poised, pretending interest, and I whisper embarrassed protest. But Mom won't be stopped. She puts a hand on mine and says, "No, darling. I have a right to crow. We've worked hard, the two of us, to get you this far."

The Perrier comes, and the waiter fills our glasses. Mom clinks hers with mine, her face radiant. "Here's to you, honey! To your bright future. To a long-run series. To all your dreams coming true!"

My face burns at her words; her dream is not mine, and I think this is the time to speak up. But instead I smile feebly and clink glasses in my toast to her. And for the rest of the lunch we reminisce about the good and bad times. The time Mom and I both had flu, and the two of us, flushed with fever, went down to the kitchen at the same time, each intending to take lemonade up to the other. The time I spent all my allowance for six months on some special stamps Mom wanted for her collection. The time I became a woman, biologically, and the closeness that developed between us as Mom explained menstruation and how babies are born.

Slightly giddy, we leave the restaurant arm in arm, whispering and laughing. I love her so much. I ache at the thought of leaving her; she's as much a part of my life as I am of hers. But it's time to cut the cord.

And I don't have the courage to tell her.

The next day she comes home jubilant. She spent the whole day on Rodeo Drive, shopping for me. She triumphantly unwraps a five-hundred-dollar silk dress, a three-hundred-dollar leather purse, and a thousand-dollar ultrasuede coat.

"Mom!" I cry. "I don't want these things!" How can she spend *my* money without even asking if it's what I want or need? Yet I feel guilty, because she's acting out of love and the belief that nothing has changed.

"Don't be silly, Val! You'll be going out to some of the most elegant places now. Come on. Try this on!"

"Take them back! I don't need them!"

Startled, Mom hesitates, and her eyes open wide. For a second I see the old fire begin to burn, but it subsides. Is it possible that she's scared of me? Have our positions switched just because of my earning power? Suddenly she seems smaller, less self-assured. Without a word of protest she starts folding the dress back into its box, lips pressed together in puzzled disappointment.

And even now I haven't the courage to explain.

The week passes quickly, and still I can't bring up the subject. With each day I become more guilty, more irritable. Even Mom notices, but she excuses it as my "needing a rest."

It's the day before Josh's deadline. I come in from an evening with Tom during which all we talk about is how to tell Mom. I am in my room going over the scenario in my head when she calls me to her room.

I'm used to seeing her at her worktable sorting stamps, but this time the table is covered with colorful brochures.

"Sit down." Her face flushes with excitement.

I sit on her bed. I have a funny feeling about what she's going to say.

"Next week we're flying to Athens and taking a cruise on the Mediterranean to Míkonos and Santoríni and—

127

Look." She holds a brochure out to me.

The pamphlet shows pictures of brilliant white houses sparkling in the sun against an unbelievably blue sky. There are pictures of people swimming in a pool on a ship or dancing at night to music played by Greek musicians. It's a dream vacation. Only I don't want to go. It means being away from Tom these last few weeks before he leaves for Stanford.

"Don't you have anything to say?" Mom asks. "We can leave next week! I've already put a deposit down. I told you we'd go abroad if everything turned out the way we hoped. You need the rest, and you'll love it. Greece is a young person's paradise. It's full of sunshine and romance."

"Young people who travel in Greece go by ferry, not cruise ships," I say irritably.

"What difference does it make? Isn't a cruise ship better?"

"Young people who travel in Greece are usually backpacking, sleeping in hostels, on the beach—"

"Pish-posh." Mom throws up her hands in dismissal. "For two weeks you don't have to live like a peasant. You can be a princess."

"It'll cost a fortune!"

"What's money? We don't have to pinch pennies anymore! You'll be making enough to do anything you ever wanted to do!"

Of all the unimportant objections I've raised so far, I finally blurt out the only one that really matters: *"Don't you think you should have asked me first?"*

This stops Mom. She puts a hand over her mouth. I can see a dozen questions flashing in her eyes: *Since*

*when do you talk to me that way? Since when do I have
to ask you first?*

"What's going on here, Valerie?" she asks at last. "Is
there something you're not telling me? I'm not your
mother for seventeen years without knowing when my
daughter is hiding something."

"It's only six episodes! We can't go splurging just on
the chance of more. . . . And Tom—"

Mom interrupts. "Don't give me this about Tom. He's
only going to Stanford. That's not so far. You can fly to
Palo Alto in an hour. And anyway, he can do without
you for two weeks. It won't kill him. He should be glad
for you." She pauses. "Out with it, Val." She sits there,
arms crossed, waiting, and I know there's no more post-
poning. My hands get moist, and my throat has a big
lump in it.

"I won't be near Palo Alto," I say almost in a whisper.
"Or L.A. I'll be in New York. I'm going to Cornell."

"Oh." Mom's eyes cloud, and she looks away. I want
to go to her and put my arms around her, but there's a
warning in her posture that holds me back.

"When did you decide this?"

"A couple of weeks ago. Mom . . ."

"Why didn't you tell me then?"

"I didn't tell you because I wasn't sure if I'd change
my mind. And I didn't want to upset you."

"I see."

"Mom, please!" I beg. "Don't make me feel worse
than I already do."

"Why?" she asks, ignoring my entreaty. "So you can
be near your father?"

"What? No! At least not only that!"

129

"Have you told him yet?"

"Of course not! I'd never do that!"

Now that I've answered her most pressing questions, the real battle starts. "How can you do this to me, Val?" she demands. "How can you?"

"Do it to *you?* I'm not doing anything to you! I'm doing it for me! Don't you understand?"

She ignores me and hurries on. "All these years we worked together. All those hours I put into your career. All those things I denied myself! I could have remarried. I could have had a career too. But no. It was all for you!"

"For *me?* It was for you, Mom! I never asked you to sacrifice everything. You never once asked me if being an actress was what I wanted! And you're only thirty-five. That's not old! Why can't you—"

Mom cuts me off. "And what about Maurie and all *he's* done for you!"

"I'm staying for the six episodes, then they can write me out. Or maybe I can do some of the episodes during vacations . . . Christmas . . .Easter . . ." I'm crying now, hungry for her approval and understanding.

"All you think about is yourself! Do you realize what a position you're putting Maurie in?"

"Josh says—"

"Josh . . . he's still wet behind the ears. What does *he* know? And what do you know? College! If you want college so much, you could go nights to UCLA or USC!"

"No!"

"Why?"

"Because I want to be on my own for a change!"

"Ah-ha! It's me you want to get away from. Your own

130

mother! Is *that* it?"

"Stop it! Stop it!" I cover my ears with my hands. "I can't stand it!" I get up and run to the door. "I don't care what you say! I'm going to Cornell! And if you don't give me your blessing, I'll go anyway!" I leave her room and slam the door, sobbing as I rush to my own room and fall on my bed.

She's an octopus. Her tentacles squeeze every inch of me. Pull one off and another grabs hold. When will she let go? Am I to be her little girl, her "property," until I'm old and gray? If she cares as much as she always says, why can't she understand?

With tears sliding down my face, I get up and walk restlessly around the room. Beyond my room is silence. She won't give in. Not Mom. She's too used to getting her way. Then what do I do?

On impulse I go to the closet and take down a suitcase. It's time to cut the strings. I'll move out. I'm not going to stay here in a constant state of war, being made to feel stupid and guilty and selfish all the time! Josh will advance me some money. I'll find my own place!

There's a timid knock at my door, and when I don't answer, the door opens. Mom stands there, red-eyed and pale, but I have no sympathy. I put the suitcase on the bed and open it.

"Val . . ." Mom says. She opens her arms to me.

I go to my dresser and take out some clothes.

"What are you doing?" she cries in alarm.

"Packing. What does it look like?"

"Val, please! Don't do this!" She rushes to the bed, slams the suitcase shut, and stands with her back

131

guarding it. "Listen to me!"

"I've heard you. I've heard you every day of my life. I'm sick of listening to you! You never listen to *me!*"

"Please, darling. Stop this. You're tearing me to pieces. I'm sorry. I'm sorry. You're right. You're one hundred percent right! I'm too protective. I'm hanging on just like all those mothers I always hate! Forgive me!"

Is it a trick? What is she up to? My heart is hammering so hard, I'm shaking.

"Listen to me! I made this mistake before. I boxed your father in with an ultimatum. 'Stay in California, or go and never see Valerie again!' It was stupid! I lost him for good, and I was too proud to back down. What difference would it have made to go east with him and give him a chance at his own dream? I don't want to make the same mistake twice!"

"What are you saying, Mom? Does this mean you won't oppose me? You'll give me your blessings?"

"If this is what you truly want, go . . ."

"Oh, Mom!" I rush to her and give her an enormous hug. Tears spill down my face. "We'll burn up the phone lines. I'll telephone you every night!"

"Phone calls are expensive," she says, always the practical one. "Unless you call after eleven when the rates go down!"

I laugh and tell her about my talk with Josh. About his promise to bring me back during the year for small jobs so we'll be able to see each other now and then.

She's subdued, trying hard to show more enthusiasm than she feels. "Maybe it's time to find out who I am too. I'll get a better job. I'm pretty smart!"

"You are! You are!" I say. "Maybe Maurie could use you."

The thought lies between us, newborn and hopeful, and we leave it at that. Mom's face is flushed now, and the wheels are turning again. "Are you sure you don't want to go to Greece?" she asks, watching me for signs of weakening.

"Yes!"

"Okay. Don't get upset! So let's talk about your college wardrobe. I'll start looking for winter things. It's going to be cold there in winter."

"*I'll* look for what I want."

A frown of pain crosses Mom's brow.

"We'll *both* go shopping," I add.

"We have relatives in Syracuse," Mom exclaims. "Wait. I'll go get their address! And maybe I can come visit you there . . ."

"*Mom!*"

"Val, Val." Mom clucks in sad acceptance.

It's going to be all right. I'll have to be on guard all the time because Mom will be in there pitching at the slightest sign of weakness. But that's all right. It's time I learn to stand up for myself.

Mom will make it. She's tough as nails and resilient as a rubber ball.

And me?

That's what I'm going to find out.

ABOUT THE AUTHOR

GLORIA D. MIKLOWITZ is the author of many books for contemporary teenagers, including *Did You Hear What Happened to Andrea?*, *The Love Bombers*, *Close to the Edge*, and *The Day the Senior Class Got Married*. Her most recent book for Delacorte Press was *The War Between the Classes*. She teaches writing at Pasadena City College and lives in La Canada, California, with her family.